DIANA GARLINGTON

SHE
WASN'T THE ONE

She Wasn't the One
Diana Garlington

ISBN: 978-1-7350328-0-1

Printed in the United States of America

Diana Garlington is represented by T. Fielding-Lowe Media Company

T. Fielding-Lowe Company, Publisher
https://www.tfieldinglowecompany.com

ACKNOWLEDGMENTS

Writing my first book was filled with many challenges and different emotions; laughter, pain, strength, and courage. I could not have done it alone. This book was a product of so many individuals' love and guidance.

My everlasting gratitude first goes to my mentor, friend, and inspiration, Kobi Dennis. I cannot recall the number of hours, sweat, tears and conversations I have shared with him in order to get me to the level of success. I have at this moment, and for what I will continue to achieve.

To my niece, Shanda Christal, for planting an everlasting memory of Esscence on November 25th, 2011.

To Arthur Johnson, who is a brother of peace, love, and blessings to my entire life of friendship. Never a judgment or fault in 35 plus years.

To Helen Baskerville - Dukes, my sister who never wavered her faith in me or my visions to bring this book into fruition.

To Thea Fielding Lowe, who is not just a publisher, but an inspiration who encourages nothing but great accomplishments.

To Keisha Jones, for her support in preparing my baby for her final viewing.

To KFM Leadership Group- one of the greatest groups of individuals I have ever met and built a family bond. A team filled with intelligence, love, unity, compassion, and strength.

To my friends and community who listened to my consistent cries and pleas for bringing justice to Esscence and the family.

To Randolph Cooper for giving me one of the greatest joys any mother would ever dream of bringing into the world.

To Todd Garlington, who was an indescribable presence in Esscence's life and who I will forever hold close to my heart.

To my beautiful and loving family who kept me uplifted and comforted during my most difficult moments after losing Esscence, especially the members who gave me a reason to continue my path in life; Keyonna, Lamar, Chavon, Xionna, Dwayne, Rameek, Jamont, Zaniah, Lanari, Baby Esscence, and Baby Tyler.

In memory of
Alejandro Brown Sr.
Alejandro Brown Jr.
Tyrone Collins
Robert E Denson
Esscence T. Christal (BOOPSIE)

Dedicated to
Wilbert and Gladys Graham
John Jackson
James Christal

A special dedication to Barbara Knighton, who was one of the strongest warriors I have ever met. She battled her own sickness, but never stopped fighting for Esscence and the family!

TABLE OF CONTENTS

ONE RED AND WHITE HOUSE

A big white and red house with six bedrooms in a quiet neighborhood in the Providence section called Washington Park is where I grew up with four brothers and one sister. Mom was a housewife, and Dad worked every day except Sundays. Mom was extremely strict, but dad was quiet and laid back. I was born into a family where you needed to be on the front porch before the streetlight came on. We attended Catholic schools, there was no sleeping out, and when you misbehaved, you would get a stare that would make one scared out of their wits! My mom was structured and a creature of habit. She would wake us up for school, get dress, have breakfast, go to school, return home, do our homework, go outside until dusk, eat, watch TV, and be in bed by nine every night.

As the weekend approached, it was waking up by 8 am, doing chores, and preparing for our family time. We all would play until 10 am then go down to the living room for wrestling. Eleven o'clock would roll around, my youngest brother Paul and me would prepare for our Saturday ritual. Our ritual was to go to New York System on Payton Street to purchase our 12 to 14 hot wieners, stop by our corner store, Charlie's Variety, for three 2-liter cokes and 2 gallons of water. We would arrive back home a little before noon to watch Soul Train. Once the clock hit 1 pm, we would be free to do whatever we wanted until my dad arrived home at 2.

The shiny red car would pull up in the driveway. My baby sister Barbara and I would come running down the stairs because we knew it was time to search the pockets of my dad's blue uniform for all his tips. Twenty, twenty-five, and sometimes a whole thirty dollars' worth of tips would be divided between the two of us. Looking back, you would say we were very privileged to have anywhere from ten to fifteen dollars of dad's tips plus an allowance of fifty dollars every Saturday to go shopping.

Weekends were set aside for the family to spend time together. Saturday afternoons around 4 pm, dad would be ready to take his drive. Barbara and I would call across the street to see if our sister from another mother could go to Quonset, where my dad would go shopping at the commissary, where he used to be stationed while serving in the US Navy. The drive was so exciting because we were getting away from the house and playing our license plate game during the trip. We would all have notebooks and pencils to see how many plates we could write down. The winner would get a dollar worth of snacks when we returned home. Turning down Indiana Avenue, we would spot our mother and our best friend, Jennifer's mom, sitting, laughing, and smoking on the front porch.

Sundays would be different. Sundays to my family were like the unscripted version of Soul Food. The family would arrive one by one while mom was in the kitchen for hours preparing her southern-style meal. With mom and dad born and raised in the South, we were raised with traditional southern values than many other neighborhood children. We were all about family first.

GOODBYE MOMMY

A few years later, as I entered middle school, a life-changing event would hit the family and introduce me to living life without a mom at an exceedingly early age. My mother was diagnosed with cancer, leaving me to grow up extremely fast to help my father raise my baby sister.

My mornings would begin by waking up one hour earlier to help mom. I would brush her hair, bathe, and dress her for the day, in addition to giving her medication. I did all of this before getting my sister Barbara and me ready for school. When we arrived home from school, I would sit with my sister and do my homework. Then be off to sit with mom telling her all about the things I could not wait to do with her. I was still not accepting that mom had cancer and believed that she had a long life to live.

It was December 28th at 8:15 in the morning. I woke up to my father holding my mother with tears dropping from his eyes.

"Daddy, what is wrong? "Why are you crying and holding mom?"

"I need you to call your brothers now." "I just called an ambulance. Mommy is not doing well!"

Very shocked and hysterical, I called the family. I remember my mother grabbing my hands and softly speaking, "You have to promise me that you will take good care of your baby sister Barbara for me."

"Mommy, please don't say that. Are you okay?"

"It's time, baby." "Mommy has to go home to heaven, but you have your father who will be here to take care of you!"

"Daddy, please tell mommy not to go!" "Please, Daddy!"

I begin to hear sirens coming down the street, growing louder and louder. I ran into a corner and began to cry hysterically while watching men in uniforms put mommy on a stretcher and take her out of the house.

We arrive at the hospital with my family to say our final goodbye to my dear mommy as she passes on with me holding her hand along with her best friend, who I called my Aunt Ruth, holding the other hand. John, my oldest brother, just continued to pace the room, crying hysterically, and begging for our mother to come back.

DIANA

Beginning the path to young adulthood, I started at Hope High School, where I would receive straight A's on my report card and get the nickname "Diana the Nerd" for the entire freshmen year of school. As time went on, I passed the 9th grade, and I entered my sophomore year. It was time for me to be the new and improved cool Diana! Still getting straight A's, I would occasionally skip class to hang out in the stairwell with the other girls. Also, I would take an interest in a senior they called Pluck.

Fifteen years old and now dating Pluck, I would begin to sneak off to our local community center to meet him. We would somehow become one of the most famous couples in school. My boyfriend was known primarily for being able to kick and jump in the air. He was called the black Bruce Lee. He was able to roundhouse and punch his adversary in a flash of an eye.

In April, during my junior year, I was sitting in the kitchen preparing a book report. I began to get a weird feeling that I had never felt before. Suddenly, I was vomiting a yellowish-colored liquid repeatedly. I go to my room, lie down, and think to myself, "my goodness, I only ate a burger. Why would I be feeling so nauseous? A few hours later, I decided to go back to the kitchen to prepare dinner, but I still felt a little nauseous.

The following day, I would go through the same cycle. I would eat then vomit, leaving myself lightheaded. Finally, I decided to call my sister-in-law to see if she could help me figure out what could be ailing me.

"Hi Denise, can I ask you something?"

"Of course."

"I keep vomiting after I eat, but it's yellowish, and I am feeling dizzy."

"Okay. Are you and Pluck having sex?"

"Why? Omg!!! Am I pregnant?"

With a short pause, she said, "It sounds like you are."

"Oh, my gosh." "Daddy is going to hate me." "What am I going to do?"

Life has changed, and I am going to be a mother! Seventeen years old with my first child and having two more by the age of 22.

THE STRIP

In the summer of 2010, I received a letter from Providence Housing stating that an apartment had become available. By this time, I was ready to move out and be on my own. I had already felt that it was time for me to be independent, move out and raise my children.

Now that I am living in my new apartment, I began hanging out with a few female friends. We would walk up and down a section of Chad Brown called "The Strip." One evening, I needed something from the store. I strolled down "The Strip" and heard a voice say, "Hey, are you the new girl over here." I continued to walk as if I could not hear anything. Again, the same voice asked, "Hey, are you the new girl over here." I proceeded to the store. On my way back, a 220lb African American man, who looked much older than me, came and said, "So you want to act stuck up, huh?!"

I responded, "No, and I am not trying to meet anyone." This man was very persistent and smooth because he finally talked me into letting him walk me to my apartment, leaving with my number in hand.

The next day, he called and said, "Hey, my sister is going away for a few days." "I want you to come visits me and let me cook your dinner." Of course, this was flattering. I was 23 and still upset that I had been cheated on and dismissed by my ex.

I get to the apartment, and he says, "I never got your name."

"Diana." "And yours?"

"Choppa, but you can call me Chop." There was a lot of laughter. Then Chop asked the age question. I told him I was 23. With more laughter, he responded, 34! I immediately thought to myself, "Diana, what are you thinking?"

Continuing with the night, I completely forgot about the age factor. I enjoyed myself so much so that I woke up the next morning after sleeping with this man. Thinking to myself, this was so dumb of you to sleep with this older man so quickly in such a short amount of time knowing him!

CELEBRATION OR DEVASTATION

It is on the 4th of July. A friend says, "Hey, let's go to the south-side of Providence."

I replied, "why not?"

I get dressed. We head out of the house. After a 45-minute walk from Chad Brown. The three of us finally arrive at our favorite hangout spot, Rhodes Street. Laughing and chatting while sitting on a wall, a friend shows up at the location with my favorite drink. I sip once, then take a second. It is an immediate feeling of nausea. Suddenly, I begin to feel very faint, with large drops of sweat rolling down my forehead. Holding my head in my hands and speaking in a low voice, I said to my female friend, "I feel like I'm going to pass out."

"You know it's hot, and we are out here drinking this liquor in the heat."

I responded, "No, it's a weird feeling!"

Gloria suggested that we go to her house, being that she lived nearby.
Entering her house, Gloria says, "Mom, you know Diana, right?"
"Of course," she replied.
Gloria tells her mom that she would let me lie on her bed for a bit, just to see if I feel better. As I walked into her room, here it comes. Vomit everywhere.

After about an hour of lying down, Gloria's mother insisted I visit the hospital approximately three blocks away. Denise and Gloria accompany me to the hospital, patiently waiting but very eager to hear the results.

After about 2 hours of blood work and urine in the cup, the doctor comes in the room and asks, "Do you have children?" I look at him with wide-open eyes and an instant attitude. "Yes." "Why would you want to know that information?" "My children are at home with my father, so if I drank too much, it should not be a problem."

He says, "I am asking you because you are pregnant and not intoxicated!"

"OMG!" "I don't believe I am pregnant!"

Fifteen minutes later, I return to the waiting area where my friends are waiting in shock and awe. I guess the look on my face was not a good one because my friends immediately jumped up and asked, "what is wrong?"

In shock, I respond, "I am pregnant." I begin to cry beyond control. They laughed and spoke. "Girl, it's all good." "We got you, and you will be okay!"

After leaving the hospital, we finally arrived back in the Chad Brown housing complex an hour or so. I silently sat with tears, thinking about telling Choppa I was not pregnant with his child.

BABY ON THE WAY

A month or so later, we are in deep conversation. Choppa was sitting on the bed with a bunch of little bags of what I assumed to be drugs. He gets a call to meet someone outside. As soon as he leaves the apartment, I grabbed one of the little bags to see what was inside. The bag was not tightly secured, so a white substance spill out. I hear footsteps entering the apartment, so I quickly throw the little bag back into the large brown paper bag and lay back down on the bed. He grabs the brown paper bag and heads back down the stairs.

A short while later, he comes back into the bedroom and says, "One of my bags was open." "You better not be doing drugs!" Pissed and in shock, a huge shouting match starts. The ridicule and accusations made me so angry that I wanted out of his presence and out of this so-called relationship. He continues, "you have that crack headed friend of yours living here, so you are probably getting high too!" With a combination of pregnancy hormones and being fed up with the nonsense of the relationship, I told Choppa that this was it, goodbye and fuck you!"

After living in the housing complex a few more months and being stressed due to the drama that took place months before, I decided to move out and relocate back to my father's residence. A couple of weeks later, I found out that a friend of mine named Tonya was also pregnant and due at the same time. Neither one of our baby's fathers were involved. Over the course of our pregnancy, we helped each other get through.

ESSCENCE

On April Fool's Day, I called my childhood friend Jennifer and said to her, "I think I may be experiencing contractions." "I want this to be a smooth pregnancy." We walked up and down Broad Street to Prairie Avenue for approximately two hours. The doctor said that walking would help with the labor. The contractions during the walk would become more assertive but then slow down. On our way home, I hoped that my water would break, but to no avail. During the night, my contractions became much more robust. By 7 am, water was immensely running down my leg. It was time to go to the hospital. After four pushes and no Choppa insight, my baby was born.

Esscence was born on April 2nd, 1990, at 9:22 am. She was 9 lbs. and 8 oz. As I lay in bed that night, I was very emotional. I was upset that her father did not see her come into the world. The next morning, the nurse came into my hospital room to fill out the baby's name forms. I thought and thought. After a quick look over on the table where they place your daily meals was an Essence magazine in bright red letters. That is it! I would name my daughter Esscence, but I would spell her name with an extra c. Tyler would become her middle name because Tyler Collins was singing on tv. Esscence Tyler Christal would be my new bundle of joy.

The following day, I was released from the hospital. When I arrived home, all the kids were thrilled and ready to meet their new baby sister, Esscence.

Baby Picture of Esscence

THE VISIT

A few days later, feeling a little hungry, I headed to the corner store to get some snacks. When walking down the street, a black car pulls alongside me. It was Essence's dad, Choppa.

"Where are you walking to, and what happened to your belly?" "You had the baby?"

A bit shocked, I said to Choppa, "I assumed your sister told you that you were the father."

"Am I?"

"Uhhh, yes." "You were nowhere to be found."

"I wasn't that hard to find."" I live right there." With a look of shock, I cannot believe her father was living just a few houses away from where I was residing with my best friend, Tonya.

"Well, what did you have, and please bring the baby by to see my mother."

"I had a baby girl, and her name is Esscence."

"Ok. "When you come from the store, bring Esscence to my house."

Continuing with my walk to the store, I began to have mixed feelings. Did I want to go and take my baby for a visit to a family that I knew nothing about? Also, currently, I was dating a man that I had previously been in a back-and-forth relationship. I was thinking hard if I wanted to take the step of involving Choppa in our lives at that moment. Quickly snapping out of it, I remembered my daughter's needs. She would need to have her biological father be part of her life too.

After arriving back at the house, I said to Tonya, "you will not believe who I just ran into!"

"Who?"

"Choppa!" "He wants his mother and himself to see Esscence." "What should I do?"

"He is the father." "He should be able to see her." "He sounds like he wants to be in her life." "Besides, she looks just like him." "When he sees how beautiful she is, he is going to fall in love."

Still very hurt that he was not present at the hospital, I proceeded to get her dressed and ready for her first visit to meet her father and his family. I slowly walked the front steps then ringing the bell on the right side. "Who is it?" yells a woman's voice from the second floor.

I respond, "Hi, my name is Diana." "Choppa asked me to come over to talk with you and the family."

"Hold on."

A young child comes down from the second floor, opens the door, and says, "My grandmother said to come up to the second floor." Spotting Choppa's car in the yard, my heart begins to beat faster and faster as I entered the house. "Oh, so you are the woman who had Randolph's baby?"

"Yes, ma'am."

"Take y'all coats off and have a seat." I removed Essence's jacket. The look on his mother's face was a look of instant love and joy.

"Oh, my!" "Randolph, this baby looks just like your sister Kim." I was not sure of who Kim was, I took a nice breath of air, and my heart began to slow down.

"What's her name?"

"Esscence," I replied.

"Boy, is she a beautiful baby?" "Choppa, tell your sister to come here."

A few moments go by, and I look over. Choppa is carefully examining her features and looking at Esscence with a slight smile.

"Well, I guess you got another grandbaby, Mom."

"Yeah, you are too old to keep bringing me grandbabies, Choppa." We all giggle in unison.

A sister whom I do not know enters the room. I assume that this must be Kim. My baby was an identical smaller version of her.

"Whose baby is that ma?"

"Well, Randolph done brought me another grandbaby." "Her name is Esscence, and your twin!"

"Oh my gosh!" "She is my twin." "Wow, so you must be the mother."

"Yes, and I apologize." "My name is Diana."

I took another quick look over to Choppa. He was still observing and smiling at Esscence. He was truly in love with his new baby daughter.

"Choppa, she looks mighty young," said his mother.

I take a moment to pause and swallow before I said, "I am 23."

"I knew you looked like a young one."

Choppa looks over to his mother and smiles with a loud giggle. Aunty Kim picks up Esscence and walks towards a door that led to another floor of the house.

"I will be right back," Kim said.

I patiently sit, waiting for my baby to be brought back to me. A short while later, another female enters the room and says, "Hi, I am another aunty to your baby." Tammie would be somewhat familiar to me, but I could not figure out why. Later, I realized that we attended the same school. After visiting for over three or so hours, I decided it was time to head home. Esscence would be accepted and be part of her new family.

MOTHERHOOD

During this time, I began to go through spats of depression. I had four children and was unsure of what direction my life was headed. Although Esscence was well taken care of by Choppa, I still felt like there was not enough effort being brought forth for me to get my life on track. I was hoping to build a family relationship with him, but that did not happen. I feel as though that kept me from getting my life on track.

Esscence was a happy and loving baby. Now at six months old, she had grown from 9lbs to 16lbs of chunky baby fat. She was sitting up without assistance from anyone. Her first tooth was breaking through her gums. I felt like it was time for her second round of baby photos with the photographer.

At nine months of age, I was sitting on the floor watching Barney on tv with her. Just for kicks, I decided to stand her up on her feet to see if she would begin walking. I did not think she would walk, but I thought I would give it a try. A couple more weeks went by, and to my surprise, Esscence took a couple of steps and drops to the floor! Shocked and delighted, I picked her up and positioned her feet. She took two more steps, wobbled, and another step. This pattern continued throughout the day. A few days later, my little one is smiling happily with two teeth and walking!

Happy First Birthday, Essence! Still a happy baby and an excited, proud mom, she was now one year old. At this age, I felt safe to enroll her in daycare. Also, I decided to begin a new chapter of my life and enroll in school. I started a program for legal secretarial studies at Katherine Gibbs. Besides, working at night as a telemarketer at Domestic Bank.

At four years old, Esscence was such a bright child. One day, Choppa picked her up and said that he would take her for the day. When Esscence returned, she said, "Mommy, my daddy took me to Pawcatuck, and it was far." All I could do was laugh hysterically because I figured she could not correctly pronounce Pawtucket. Unknown to me, she was right. She would have visited Pawcatuck but in Connecticut and not in Rhode Island. Later, when I contacted Choppa asking where they had been that day and repeating Esscence's statement to him, he was just as shocked as I was because he had never mentioned to her where they were going. At that age, Essence was smart enough to read signs and understand distance.

Life for my family and I was coming together for us. One morning, I was sitting outside, getting some fresh air, when the mailman arrives. The envelope was addressed to me, so I placed the other mail down on the cement step, opening my letter. As I read the letter, I began to smile. I was approved for a three-bedroom apartment at Barbara Jordan Housing. By this time, Esscence would be four and ready for pre-school.

One afternoon after getting her off the bus, I decided that I would get something to drink from the corner store, Public Street Market. I walked into the store. There was a light-skinned woman with a little boy who resembled Esscence so much that it startled me. The girl said, "Is that Choppa's daughter?" I hesitated to answer but nodded yes in agreement.

She then said that "I am her big brother's girlfriend." With a sigh of relief that this was not going to be a drama-type conversation, I told her my name and asked if she could relay a message. Unfortunately, I was told that her 20-year-old brother was incarcerated. It would be sometime before he would be able to visit Esscence. She said that she would make sure he was aware of the conversation and where the information on contacting us. I would also find out that the little boy who resembled Esscence so much was her nephew.

RELOCATION

A year or so later, now dating Carlos, we decided it was time for a change of scenery. Carlos' parents were relocating to Sumter, South Carolina. We thought that a new environment would be good for the kids and us, so we moved as well. Although the kids were excited about the move to South Carolina, I was worried about leaving my father behind. My sister had moved to Florida, which would mean that he would be living in the house alone.

Esscence would be 5 ½ years old when we relocated to Sumter. Because of her intelligence and rapid development, I always felt that she would either become an actor, dancer, or a sharp-shooting lawyer. As time went on, she became the entertainer of our family. She would recite the entire lyrics to songs, dance and was just the life of the party.

While in South Carolina, we planned a birthday party for our next-door neighbor. That family was going through some hardships. They had used all their money to move into their new home. The mom was waiting for assistance, and the dad was seeking employment. Due to them not having enough money to pay their utilities, their lights were turned off. Also, they could not buy food. We decided to have the birthday party at our house, providing all the food, decorations, and entertainment to help them out.

While celebrating the birthday, we decided to play a song. Essence sang "Gangster Lean" to the father, who we were celebrating. I remember she could not pronounce homies in the song verse. Instead, she would say "hummies." Esscence would sing the whole song word for word. The neighbor was so satisfied with joy that he began to cry. She had a way of connecting with people. And you saw these connections throughout her life.

When Esscence had entered kindergarten, she was a child who would adapt to her environment quickly and be intuitive to people. I always felt that Esscence had a special gift of knowing if someone was good or evil. Not knowing how she knew about people's situations; she would make comments about their personalities. We would continuously say to her, "Esscence don't say that." But later, we would find out that her intuition was correct.

As time went on, we began to feel like Sumter was not the kind of place where we wanted to raise our children. The city was more for people who wanted to retire and settled down. Not long afterward the initial move, we relocated to Raleigh, North Carolina. Raleigh was more city-like than we were more accustomed to coming from Providence, Rhode Island.

All the kids were doing great after the move to Raleigh. They were excelling in school and meeting new friends. It was a perfect fit for the family.

HEARTBREAK

After two years of living in Raleigh, I received a call that would change everything. All our hopes of starting fresh in a new city would quickly vanish. My dad was diagnosed with cancer. Once again, I dealt that dreadful blow and now recalling hearing those very words as a young girl about my mother. Without a second thought or delay, I decided it was best for us to move back to Rhode Island. I wanted to be there for my father, to help him get through this difficult time. We were going to make sure that every day was going to be spent with fun and laughter. We were not letting the children fully understand that their grandpa was ill and may not get better.

It was summer when we relocated back to Rhode Island. We moved right into my father's house. I knew I had to live with him to handle his affairs. Although I learned the importance of caring for my father, I still had to find employment and figure out the new norm between my family's schedule and dad's care. After a conversation with Carlos, we decided that the position I had obtained as a loan officer made more money and could sustain the family. Carlos would stay home; take care of dad and the kids. The move on the kids was not hard. They jumped right back into the same routine.

On a Sunday night, Carlos and I were watching television. I remember hearing my dad entering the restroom. Within moments, there was some sort of noise that sounded like a fall coming from the bathroom. Quickly jumping up, I rushed to the bathroom and opened the door to find my father lying on the floor. I began to talk to him.

"What led him to pass out?"

In the meantime, Carlos was calling 9-1-1 as I was giving aid to my father. Later after arriving at the hospital, we would find out that the cancer was progressing, and dad was losing blood internally. After speaking with the doctors, I would receive heartbreaking information that dad had less than one month to live.

Being stubborn as my father was, he decided to return home instead of being taken to a hospice to live out the rest of his days. Continuing, enjoying the time that we had, I remember my father sitting outside in the sun while the girls and I played hopscotch, jump rope, and play jacks on the porch. My son played baseball with Carlos in the yard. As I said before, I wanted every day to be filled with smiles, but less than a month later, we would share tears of my father's passing.

A week after the hospital visit, I received a call from my boss, asking if I could come into work for a few hours or so to cover another employee's shift. I worked for about an hour when I received a call to please come home as soon as possible. My dad was not doing well. When I arrived, I was told that my father had already passed away.

Losing my father and trying to heal from the pain of his loss, the family had yet suffered another tragedy. My brother, James, had passed from diabetes one year later, the same day, 2 or 3 minutes after my father. James died on November 21st, 1999, at 9:22 am. Dad passed away on November 21st, 1998, at 9:17 am.

HIT BY A CAR

While still working and excelling in my career at a downtown law firm, Esscence was hit by a car at the age of 9 and thrown onto the car's windshield. I received the call at work, and grabbing my things in a frantic state, I jumped up, ran past my boss, and out of the building, hailing the closest cab. When I arrived, by the grace of God, she was okay. She was a little sore. Thankfully, there was no damage to her head from hitting the windshield of the vehicle.

A bizarre thing came about while being at the hospital. Ace, my two children's father, Chavon, and Lamar came into the hospital without knowing. He stated he was the father to get into her room. Soon afterward, her biological father, Choppa, would arrive at the hospital and become upset and somewhat disturbed that Ace said that he was Esscence's father.

Later, I would contact Choppa, which he would instantly brush off. He would become distant and adamant that he was no longer accepting that he was Esscence's biological father for some years after. Shocked, puzzled, and very hurt, I would try and figure out what could have possibly transpired to make him begin this charade.

One Sunday, after attending church, I contacted Choppa and asked if he would allow me to talk to him to get something off my chest. He accepted my conversation. As we sat and talked, he explained, "When I came to the hospital to check on Esscence, the nurse told me that her father had already arrived and was visiting with her."

Fueled with anger, I explained, "You know there is no possible way he could be her father. This was very childish of you to remove yourself from her life knowing that."

Slowly, he began to visit Esscence now and then but was not fully back in her life, like he once was before the accident. The summer came around; Ace informed me that he would be bringing Chavon, Lamar, and a daughter from another mother to Atlanta on vacation. He explained that he felt terrible that Esscence would be left behind and asked if she could also go. I had no problem with him bringing her with the rest of the children because he would guard her as if she were one of his children.

Less than a week later, I received a call from her father stating that he heard Esscence had accompanied Ace to Atlanta. Now he believed that Ace was possibly the father of Esscence. For weeks, we argued like cats and dogs without any change of mind. Month after month, there was not a word from him. I simply did not have the energy or the time to continue this unnecessary battle with her father, so I insisted we take a DNA test to put this to rest. After constant calls and messages, there was no effort from him to take the DNA test. He just continued to be distant and non-responsive when it came to Esscence.

GENERATIONAL CURSE

While sitting on the porch with my friend, Jenny, laughing and reminiscing while watching the kids play in the yard, the phone rings. Esscence is the first to run to pick it up. I see her begin to look as if she is going to scream or cry. She frantically says, "Mommy, please hurry up and bring me to the hospital." I am in shock and ask why!

She said, "Mommy, someone just said that Lil Honda got shot." "Please, hurry up and take me to the hospital." I run into the house, grab my purse and keys. We head out to the hospital.

Upon arrival, I see many individuals screaming, pacing, crying, and being hysterical, saying, "OMG!" "He is gone." "He is gone." Please bring him back!" I proceeded to the waiting area to find Choppa. The look that he gave me was of utter pain that I wish no parent would ever have to endure. He looks at me and says, "They killed my grandson." "He is gone!" I immediately grab Esscence, trembling, remembering the feeling when I lost my mother, father, and brother. Essence's dad would embrace her traumatically, letting her know that he loved her. He held her for a very long time without letting her go from his embrace.

The following day, I told Esscence that we would visit the family to see if there was anything I could do to help. When we arrive, Esscence gets out of the car and greets her big sister, Sparkles. After a long conversation, I tell them that I would come and check on them again the following day. Interrupting me, her sister on her dad's side says, "I would like for my baby sister to stay here with me for a while, please"! I had never left Esscence with any other family besides mine. I was a little skeptical. But I agreed, stating that I would be back to pick her up in a few hours. Later that night, I went back to pick Esscence up. From that point on, she would be close to her big sister, calling, visiting, and being a loving, faithful little sister.

GENERATIONAL CURSE

Brother #1

As I left the house on my way to the market, a black Honda Accord swerved towards my car as I began to pull off from in front of the house. I was a little nervous, but a familiar face with a big smile pulls alongside my car. It was no other than Essence's look-alike. Her big brother, Honda, was released from jail and on the prowl to find his baby sister. Honda jumps out of the car and runs to the passenger side, picking up Esscence and giving her one of the most prolonged hugs ever.

"My little sis, I miss you." "You look like you should be my daughter instead of my baby sis." He turns and says to me, "Ma, I missed you!"

"Wow, so glad to see you."

Honda said, "I will pick up the kids, and I want Ess to come with me, Ma."

"I was going to take her shopping." "When I come back, you can come to pick her up," I responded.

"Okay," he answered.

Later that evening, when I returned home, I received a call from her brother Honda.

"Ma, I am going to keep the kids tonight and wanted to keep my sister too."

"Okay, love." "But here are the rules." "Please make sure she doesn't stay anywhere else but with you." "And please don't leave her alone with anyone."

"Ma, you know I got my sister." "Nothing will happen to her when she is with me."

For months, this would become her weekend getaway. Her brother would call faithfully every Friday to spend time with his baby sister.

It is May 13th The phone rings, and it is my niece, Shanda, who I always thought of as a younger sister.

She says, "Aunty, you know Chaps be jumping?" "Aunty Barbara, you and I should go."

I loved Chaps, so I was all for it. Carlos was working nights, so I thought I would occupy my time with the girls.

There was another ring from the phone. It was Esscence's big brother, Honda. "Ma, is my baby sister ready?" "We are staying at my sister's house tonight because it's her son's birthday."

I replied, "Okay, love. "I will get her ready."

Within an hour or so, he arrives to pick up Esscence and says, "I know how you are about Esscence, so here is the address to where Sparkles lives and her phone number. I share a smile of thanks. Eight o'clock comes, and I am ready to go out with my niece and sister. Once we arrive at Chaps, it's dancing, laughing, and having a wonderful time. As 12:30 approaches, I realized it was time for me to hurry off and pick-up Carlos from work.

I pulled in front of the house to drop Carlos off and returned to the club, which did not close until 2 am. Before I pulled off, I decided to run into the house and grab a quick drink since the club prices were slightly on the high side. Before I finish the last sip of my drink, I heard screaming and a commotion coming into the house from Shanda and Barbara. They had left the club to inform me of what had transpired at the club.

"Aunty!" "Aunty!" "Hurry up!" "Please come downstairs!" "They shot him!" "I think he is dead!"

"WHAT!" "OMG!" "What the hell are you talking about?" "They shot who?" I yelled.

"Honda!"

I replied, "There is no way that that was him!" What! "No way." "He is at his sisters with Esscence." "Wait!" I screamed and began to panic. "Where is Esscence?" "He has Esscence! "Where is my baby?"

I dashed down the stairs in a panic. We all rush out of the house to head back to the club to see what was going on. People were forming crowds in the street. Cops had formed a barrier wrapping yellow tape around a car and the front and back of the building! We saw an ambulance and what appeared to be someone lying inside that had the silhouette of Honda.

I asked one of the bouncers, "What is going on"?

He replied, "Honda, his sister, and cousin were shot."

"His sister and cousin were shot too. Wait!!! Where the hell is my daughter?" "She was with her brother and sister at her house!!! Where is Esscence? Frantically, I begin yelling! "OG"! "Shanda"! "Barbara"! "Honda came and got Ess earlier." "They were supposed to be at his sister's house, so who has her?"

In all the chaos, I called her father yelling. I could not speak clearly from being so frantic. He hangs up because he is now getting notified that his oldest son, cousin, and daughter were involved in a shooting. I could finally think clearly enough to remember that he gave me the address and phone number to where they would be. I called the number, and a man answers the phone. He introduces himself as Sparkles's boyfriend. "I am Essence's mother. Is my daughter with you?"

"Yes, well, I don't know if you heard, but there has been a shooting." "Can you tell me if you are at this address, so I can come and pick up my daughter?"

"Did you say shooting? Where are her sister and brother?

"I am on my way!"

Rushing to address what was written on the piece of paper at full speed, we arrive to find that Esscence was safe.

I explained the conversation that I had earlier that day with Honda to the boyfriend. Afterward, I rushed off to the hospital. Upon arriving, I could tell that it was not looking good. Before I could get a word out, I heard those words with a scream to follow. "He is gone." This would be the start of tragedies that would leave Esscence traumatized.

GENERATIONAL CURSE

Brother #2

Tyrone, who was nicknamed Ty, was a quiet and laid-back man. He would come to visit Esscence and sit for hours just adoring his baby sister. Also, Ty had made some love connections. He dated my baby sister and had two children with her.

I can recall one day cooking in the kitchen. Esscence was sitting in the living room watching a music video featuring the female rapper, Queen Latifah. The name of the song was called "Unity." Esscence comes running into the kitchen.

"Mommy, my sister is on tv, look!"

Very puzzled, I respond," what, sister Ess?" "That is a song."

She says, "Mommy, she said U and I –T-Y. Laughing hysterically, I could not believe her thoughts. She thought Queen Latifah was her sister because she called her big brother T-Y!

Tragedy would hit again soon after Esscence experienced the passing of her brother, Honda. Still devastated and hurting, she would mourn the death of her second oldest brother, who would be cheated out of life being shot on Christmas Eve.

That evening, Ty was leaving his girlfriend's apartment in the Chad Brown housing complex with his two children, and later he would be shot. I recall the horrifying call I received from my sister, Barbara. Hearing the loudest scream that I have ever heard from her, the feeling of panic swept over me. I asked

Barbara if I could come to pick her up. I immediately rushed to my sister and began wondering about the children. I thought to myself that Tyrone was shot with the children witnessing someone taking their father's life! When I arrived at my sister Barbara's house, I found out that someone had already secured the children and got them home safely.

My sister and I headed to the hospital. Once again, we witnessed the same scenario just a short time before. The death of Esscence's second brother would be leaving us devastated and looking for answers.

MIDDLE SCHOOL

As Esscence moves into her pre-teen years, there were quite a few changes that happen. My relationship with Carlos began to diminish slowly over time. We would eventually separate. For two years, the family-focused on healing and providing support to each other to get through much heartbreak. During this time, I met and started to date Todd, who I would eventually marry. He became an instant father figure to my kids and became a blessing to the family.

Esscence, now attending middle school, begins a path of disobedience and isolation. One night after visiting a close friend, I arrived home, and my oldest daughter, Keyonna, would have a bizarre look on her face. I asked what was wrong. She gasped, and she said Esscence was going to run away because she wanted to be free from your rules. I went to her room and found a handwritten note that stated the very same words her sister told me. I immediately contacted our local police. They said they could do nothing because she had not been missing for at least 24 hours. I began to make calls and started searching every place I could think of that she had visited at one point. After staying up all night, sobbing and praying, I received a call from my close friend, Lisa, who attended high school during my teenage years. She said that her daughter also wrote the very exact words on what seemed to be the same paper as Esscence.

We began to scour the neighborhood, trying to find our daughters. Finally, we were led to a house that we had never visited. We would find that both of our girls were safe but in a stranger's house without adult supervision. We contacted our local police but were given the runaround. The police said that they could not enter the home unless a parent were home. They needed evidence that the girls were in the house. Truly angry and upset, we decided to take matters into our own hands. One kick, two kick, we yelled, "Open this door because we know that you both are in there!" After several minutes of yelling and kicking, the two girls exited the front door with sad looks on their faces. We took our daughters and went on our way. As time went on, Esscence would refocus her life and begin to attend school.

One evening, Todd says, "let's go see a movie since we have been in the house for months." After cooking dinner and giving my 16-year-old instructions, 1- no one can leave the house, 2- no one can be on the phone, and 3- no fighting. We were off to the show. After less than 45 minutes of arriving at the theatre, we received a frantic call from Keyonna saying, please come home as fast as you can. Esscence had snuck out and was involved in a car accident. The car had flipped over, and the authorities could not get her out.

I screamed, cried, and shouted all the way. It was raining that night, and the streets were slippery. Todd was driving about 90 to the house. We almost lost our lives that night because a car cut us off, which led us to hydroplane many feet. Somehow, my fiancé was able to gain control of the vehicle. When we finally arrived, my neighbor runs up to me and says Esscence was okay. We had to pry her out of the car with the "jaws of life" to get her out.

As the ambulance is getting ready to pull off with my baby, I jump in and pray, pray, and pray some more that God would please not take my baby away from me. We arrived at the hospital, but I just could not go into the room to see what she would look like from the accident. Todd went in returning and saying that my beautiful baby had blood coming from her mouth and a few teeth were missing. I immediately dropped to my knees. I felt like it was my time to leave the earth because my heart was beating immensely.

Once out of the hospital and the healing process beginning, there would be dentist appointments, specialists, etc. With Esscence being young, she began to worry that she would be laughed at in school if she had attended with teeth missing. Crying daily not to attend school, I removed her from the school roster and registered her for homeschooling. Some weeks later, we returned to her dental office, leaving with a new set of teeth and a beautiful smile.

BEST FRIEND'S DEMISE

The family was back to somewhat of our everyday life, including Esscence attending school again. At the age of 14, she would bring a new friend home and introduce me to her. Her nickname was Gunner. A little shocked by the nickname. I asked where that name originated. Neither one of them responded, so I left it alone.

I went into the kitchen to fix them all some lunch. I remember feeling that Essence was finally getting some of her life back because Gunner would become close and spend more time at the house than in the streets. I loved the relationship because I had no worries, always knowing where the girls were.

One evening, the two were playing a board game in the living room. Her friend said she was feeling a little lightheaded and having problems breathing. Immediately, I told her to contact her parents to meet me at the hospital. When we got to the hospital, Esscence pleads for me to let her stay with her friend while she is being checked. The girl's parents get to the hospital, so I decide to stay with them for support.

We sat in the hospital's waiting room for about an hour before Gunner was taken to the observation area. During that waiting time, Gunner was still complaining of difficulty of breathing. Suddenly, there was a lot of confusion and a look of distress on her parent's faces. The nurse comes to the waiting area. We were not prepared to hear the results. Esscence's best friend went into cardiac arrest a few moments after walking into the hospital evaluation room. She could not resuscitate!

I thought to myself, how am I going to stop these horrific events from occurring in my life? Worried about the family, I scheduled time for everyone to see a counselor at the Providence Center.

REBELLION

Hanging out with Chavon's sister, Shalanda, returned Esscence to a path of anger and rebellion. Esscence would hangout late after school, going to houses where there would not be any adult supervision, and skipping school on some days. After weeks of arguing and going back and forth with her, she would become more rebellious. I began to stay more involved with her everyday activities after school.

One day, she led me to the house occupied by an older female who was the Godsister to Shalanda. They would hang there because they could have male visitors. Though I told her not to go to this house, Esscence would disobey me.

After filing police reports and implementing punishments, she continued to drift off to this house. One evening, I had finally had enough of the police not being able to do anything. After speaking to the apartment renter, who was allowing the girls to do whatever they wanted, I went there and demanded that I was let in to get my daughter. I specified that I better not ever catch her there again. A mountain of words went back and forth with the renter. Keyonna and the renter got into a scuffle. After getting them under control, the cops arrived, and Esscence emerged from the apartment.

One morning, as we started our regular morning routine, we all met downstairs for breakfast. Esscence was not part of the group. I wondered why she had not joined us for breakfast as she always did before. I proceeded upstairs to her bedroom and sat on the side of her bed, asking Ess what was wrong and why she was not downstairs for breakfast? She replied she was feeling ill and wanted to know if it would be okay to stay home from school. After a few more questions about how she was feeling, I decided that she could stay home. I kissed her on the forehead and told her that I would give her a call on my break.

I arrived home from work that evening with Todd immediately saying, "If I told you something, you would have to promise not to lose it and explode." I said, please do not tell me it's what I think it is. My baby was having a baby! This was the point in my life where I became bitter, angry, and ashamed, and broken because I was a mother who had to work and could not afford to stay home to be a mom to my children. All the guilt and shame took over me, and I became ill. Constantly for two weeks, I cried myself to sleep. I cried every morning, wondering why I was being punished so badly.

In the 2nd month of her pregnancy, I began to support her as a young mom and making sure she was well-nourished. Chavon would be by her side during the entire pregnancy, making sure she was taking good care of herself.

The pregnancy was still a tough pill for me to swallow. With that, Todd would be her most significant help. I remember he used to come in and say Boops just called because she was craving nuggets and French fries. Or Esscence would tell me she forgot lunch for school. I would run to Wendy's because I would later find out that he was afraid to tell her no. After all, he was scared to get a star in his eye.

At the beginning of her eighth month, Todd and I headed to Virginia for our cousin's wedding. My oldest daughter would be staying home, so I felt it was okay for Esscence to stay home since it would be only a three-day trip. At the same time, I had so many doubts that crossed my mind. So, I just packed her and Chavon up and took them to Virginia with us.

Once we arrived in Virginia, everyone was so excited to be in such a beautiful state. They completely forgot about the long drive and wanting to be back home. I felt at peace, having her with me, just if she went into early labor or some other issue could have risen.

As we entered month number 9, I would finish preparing for my wedding day and my grandson's arrival. On July 19th at 2:40 in the morning, Todd and I heard a knock on the door. It was Esscence.

"Mommy, I think I just peed on myself." We both began to laugh.

"No, Boops." "That means your water broke, and labor is about to start." I helped her get cleaned up and ready for her delivery. Esscence was my child. I wanted to prepare her for labor. She looked at me and said, "I already know, mommy." "It's going to be a lot of pain." We contacted the father and let him know that it is now time to head to the hospital. We arrived at the hospital, and labor begins. Since the father and Chavon would be there, I decided to head to work and leave when she was ready to deliver. Patiently waiting, I decided I will head over for lunch to check on her.

MY BABY IS HAVING A BABY

The clock read 11:45, fifteen minutes before my lunch break. The phone rings and Esscence's sister said, mommy, come now. She is 8 centimeters dilated, and they are preparing for delivery. I arrived at the hospital. It is time to push and bring the little guy into the world. At 12:09, Dwayne Alan Christal entered the world weighing 7 pounds 2 ounces. I remember at that moment that all the hurt and shame went out the window. I was a grandmother. It was from my little Boops, who I had spoiled outrageously. The father's family and my family became one by the blessings of the Lord. We all would be a blessing to his life.

The night before I was to walk down the aisle, Esscence came to my room. She knocked on my door with Dwayne, his bottle, and diapers, saying I want to sleep with you tonight since this will be my last day as your baby. When she fell asleep, I could not stop the tears from falling. All I could think was, you will always be my baby, but just in another way. July 23rd, 2005 would be a new beginning for the entire family, a new grandchild, a new husband, and a new beginning.

Looking back on things, I remember Esscence begging me to pick up my now fiancé's son every weekend to spend the night with us. She was already a little polished with motherhood. She was a better mom than a lot of women who have experienced birthing many children.

That morning, I would get ready for my wedding to become Mrs. Garlington. She smiled and helped me to the very last moment before I walked down the aisle. Dwayne is now a few weeks old, and I remember getting up every four hours with her to make sure he was fed and changed. Very shocked, she would already be up doing her motherly duties. Esscence continued with school. Her boyfriend and his family would step up to assist so she could finish her high school education.

Esscence stayed in her relationship with Big Weez until Dwayne was about a year and a half. Between me and Big WEEZ's grandmother, we would take turns in helping to raise him. As time went on, his father would be his constant caretaker while Esscence was continuing school.

Esscence was almost 18 years old and was on a positive path as a new mother and adult. She was able to gain employment at a local Dunkin Donuts. Also, she would receive her settlement from the accident that happened during her early years. She was not able to obtain her settlement since she was a minor. With her first new car and her beautiful smile, she could now put that chapter behind her.

TURNING POINT

Dwayne was 2.5 years old when Essence's life would take a turn. I was working at a local hotel in downtown Providence. Every morning at 9:15 am, I would receive a call from my princess to say hello and ask how I was doing. Every day, she would receive the same answer, "Duh, I am working." I would say with a short giggle.

"Ok big head, I will see you when you get out and bring me something to eat."

" Love you."

On this day, she did not call. I phoned her sister, Chavon, and asked if she had heard from her. She stated that she had been hanging at Barbara's house all day. Later that day, I decided to visit my sister, who was living on Harvard Avenue. I remember pulling up to the house and seeing Shalanda and some other women and men sitting on the hood of a car. I exited my car and saw Esscence sitting next to an individual, who I immediately remember hearing to be bad for business.

 I approach the car she was sitting on and asked her, "why are you out here with them?"

"Why, mommy?" "What's wrong?" "That is my new friend?"

"Do you know how old he is?"

"No, but not that old." "I don't think."

"Ess, you need to stay away from him and those other guys too." "Mommy, it's not like that. We are just chilling." I proceeded to Barbara's house upset.

Over a period, I would see Boops a few times with the same individual. Continually trying to sway her to walk away, it was clear she wanted to be involved with this individual. Shortly afterward, the calls started coming in, warning me that he would be a problem for Esscence. I was her mother, but she was now an adult with a child, so what could I do?

I began to get so frustrated knowing that she would be involved with this guy that I would almost make myself sick. Something said, "Diana, you have to let her find out on her own and pray that it is sooner than later." Slowly with caution, I began to stop the chastising of her being involved and just prayed for the best.

Things would not get any better. One night, I was lying in bed, and I heard some sort of scuffle going on upstairs, where Esscence decided to move her bedroom. I quietly listened and heard, "Smurf, get the fuck off me! "Don't you ever try to spit on me again!" "Don't get mad because I know you were at that bitch's house!"

"Whatever."

I quickly walked up the stairs. "Esscence, what is going on?" "I know he didn't hit you and try to spit on you!" Shocked looks came from both. "Did you just try to spit on her?"

With an exceedingly long pause and an instant snap, I headed back down the stairs quickly to my room, slamming my door leading to my closet.

"What is wrong?" Todd yells. "Why are you going to that closet? "

There was no response from me.

"Diana, why are you in that closet?"

"He hit and tried to spit on Esscence."

He quickly follows me, saying, "Don't you do that!" He grabs the gun. "Are you crazy?" "Are you trying to lose everything and go to jail?" "Let it go!"

"Get him out of this house before I flip the fuck out!"

He heads down the stairs while I shouted, "if you ever touch or try to spit on my baby again, I will kill you."

"Whatever, man," Smurf said. He leaves out the door.

Frustrated and talking to myself about doing the wrong thing, I called the police department, stating that an individual is known in the streets as "Smurf" just hit and spit at my daughter. I tell them that I would like to put it on record that if he ever does this to my daughter Esscence again, I will shoot him. The officer quickly interrupts me saying, "Ma'am, you are being recorded during this call."

"Yes, I know. "

"Calm down; we are sending someone right over." The officer asked, "Did you say Smurf because you should try hard to get your daughter away from him." "Are you armed right now?"

"Yes. The gun is registered and is no longer in my possession."

"Where is he now?"

"He just left!"

"Stay away from him and keep calm." "Someone is on the way now."

The officer arrives moments later, and of course, Esscence will not pursue charges or an arrest. The officer quickly states, "Ma'am, please refrain from ever calling the police and using the word gun, especially as frantic as you were because this could have turned pretty ugly!"

"Do you have a daughter that was spit on and hit?"

"No!"

"Okay then."

"That's what we are here for."

"Well, that's crazy cause he just walked away!"

The officer left our house.

I turned to Essence, saying, "Esscence, you know how I feel about my kids." "Why would you let him get away with disrespecting you like that?"

"Mom, it's okay." "Please calm down! Essences said.

"You will either get hurt." "It is going to be him or me if you continue to let this happen."

THE DRAMA CONTINUES

A couple of weeks later, the phone calls, the fighting, and the drama have continued. It began to get so out of hand; I would start thinking of what I could do to get her away from him and out of that relationship. I would call her daily and tell her that I wanted to spend time with her and my other children on the weekends. She would agree because this would be the time that Smurf would perform his disappearing acts.

I recall taking her out one night to Club 650. I was sitting at a table happy and giggly with her and her sister, Chavon. There was a familiar face that I thought I knew, walks into the club, and gives Esscence a real weird stare. I asked who she was because I could not quite remember her. But thinking at the same time, did I want to know who she was because it could lead to drama. It was a girl who was dating Smurf at the same time, along with two other women. Afterwords were exchanged, and the tension subsided; one of the girl's friends said to me, "Who would be out with their young daughter anyway?" After a brief exchange of words, she gets involved calming down the chaos and leading the ladies to exit the establishment.

I talked to Esscence, telling her my thoughts on her still carrying on with Smurf due to her continually encountering issues. Instances like this would continue for many months, but I had a plan and was not changing it for anyone. I was doing a good job keeping her occupied for some time, but it soon began to fade because of the guilt from what was said by the girl who had the altercation at the club.

One Saturday afternoon, I was sitting home because Todd would be hanging out with his boys. My sister Barbara called to say they would cook and have a few drinks at Gibbs' cousin's house. They wanted me to come hangs out. After a while of procrastinating, I get dressed and head over to the house. I am having a good time sitting outside with my chair when a car drives up. At first, the car moves slowly, but I see the reverse lights come on, and the vehicle starts rolling backward within moments. An individual, who I knew since he was about 11 years old, says, "Ain't you Lamar's mom?' I gave the young guy a sarcastic chuckle because he knew who I was. Not only that, but I had already heard there was an incident that took place in an elevator at court with Esscence, Smurf, and this individual. I continued to tell this boy sarcastically, "you know who I am." I used to wipe your dirty ass nose when you were riding bikes with Lamar, remember."

After a very pissed look, he sarcastically states, "Well, tell Esscence to stay out of the car with him." "Cause we got problems."

The car pulls off quickly. I immediately call her outside and explain what happened. Very sternly stating, "So how do you see why I said keep your ass out of the car and away from him?"

"I know, mom."

Upset and aggravated, I state that I am ready to go home.

THE APARTMENT

My words would quickly go in one ear and ultimately out the other. The weekend approached, and Esscence would be upstairs with her sisters Chavon and Keyonna, her boyfriend Smurf, and his cousin Lennie. They would be roasting sessions and laughter with all of them for hours. The following Saturday afternoon, Esscence approached me asking if I could bring her to an agency to look for an apartment. About a week or so after, she would come in smiling, saying, "Mommy, I got my first apartment." "Sissy is moving in with me." I was a little sad, but happy. She was moving on in adulthood.

The big day came, and we moved here and Chavon into their new apartment. Weeks went by, and I would continue visiting and praising the girls for their independence. Those praises would soon quickly change to become concerned questions. I was continually praying that Esscence would stay on the right path, seeing she had past troubles with Smurf and the girls. But she did not!

The phone rings. "Mommy, someone kicked-in my door and stole all of Weezy's (Esscence's son Dwayne) and my clothes, CDs, videos, and food." "The clothes that were left were bleached." "Also, they broke my tv."

Pissed and frustrated, I got into my car and headed over to their apartment. I witnessed exactly what she described over the phone. I began asking questions about her dealings and who could have done this. I explained to her that a police report would need to be filed.

A few days later, we would find out that Lennie, who visited the house, would be one of the individuals involved in the criminal acts at her apartment. He kicked in the door for girls who had a personal vendetta against Esscence. Knowing the temperament, Esscence had, I forewarned her not to retaliate.

"Mommy, I can't let them get away with doing that. If it was just my stuff, maybe, but they destroyed my son's property too. Quickly interrupting, I said, "Esscence, I will purchase you and my grandson all new clothes and replace your other things.

"Sorry, Mommy, I don't want you to have to take care of me anymore. I am grown with a child."

A day or two later, I received a call that Esscence was on a local street named Burnett Street, where her cousin, Dominique, resided. Dominique said Esscence was getting ready to approach the girls who destroyed her and her son's clothes, stole their food and other items. I immediately rushed over to Burnett Street in my car, jumping out, trying to coerce Esscence to let it go. Deep in my heart, I already knew that this issue would not be left alone. Standing in her face, continuously trying to calm her down, I turned around and saw Ronda, whose family I knew well. I quickly said, "You have to be kidding me." "Are you trying to fight my daughter, and you're a grown-ass woman." "I don't think so!" Words of disrespect were directed at me. That was the beginning of the fight. I see Esscence charge at her. This would go on for a few moments, with nearly 25 to 30 individuals cheering the battle to continue. I stepped in to disrupt the fight while another brother begins spewing, "You old as Bitch." "I will fuck you up if you don't let it continue.

For an instant moment, a shouting match began between him and me. It ended as the police start pulling up. We were quickly dispersed with a police report being filed. I proceeded to take Esscence and her sister back to my house to let things die down. She returned home later that evening.

A few months later, Esscence had to put her vehicle in the shop. She asked for a ride to pay her rent. Upon arrival, she noticed a look of frustration because she had Smurf waiting there with her. She knew I would cringe at the thought of her still entertaining this monster: I, Todd, her, and the monster headed to the office to pay her rent. While sitting and waiting, Esscence rushes out the door with him following. "Mommy," with a high tone, "can you please drop him off near Hanover Street?" "His cousin was in an altercation." Hanover Street being 3 to 5 minutes away, I proceed to drop him off and then went back to pick up Esscence.

Arriving back to the office to get Esscence, she was crying and very distraught and screaming.

"What is wrong?" with a low-pitched voice.

"Mommy." "They shot him."

"Who, Esscence?" "Who?"

"They shot his cousin, and he is dead!"

In dismay," I just left and didn't see anyone fighting."

"He died, Mommy." "Can you bring me to the hospital?"

Once again, arriving at the hospital, we found out that he had died. For the next couple of days, we heard disturbing things about what transpired while Smurf was at the scene with his dying cousin. There were rumors that he had taken money and keys from his dying cousin's pocket. He was then going to his cousin's apartment where he lived and stealing his belongings.

I began telling Esscence, "I am begging you to get away from him." "His flesh and blood are saying that he did this to his cousin." "He will do the same to you!"

"I know, Mommy."

"I hope it is not true. Because although we found out that Lennie kicked-in my door, I would not wish bad luck like that on anyone. Smurf and Lennie were not talking that much. Because we found out that Lennie was the one who had kicked in the door, but I don't think he is that grimy."

"That monster does not give two shits about you or anyone!"

The more I would try to separate her from him; it seemed as though he would become more involved. She would begin hanging with her boyfriend's sister, Mama, whom I feel would be her distraction to continue with his secret rendezvous with the 4 to 5 other women.

MORE BAD COMPANY

Everyday Esscence and Mama would be in the house hanging out in the computer room. One night, I had received a Louis Vuitton bathing suit for myself and a Burberry bathing suit for Esscence. We had been showing the girls how to make flyers when I opened the package.

The following day, I was excited to show Todd that I had received the swimsuit in the mail. I was looking all over the room, asking, and trying to recall where I put it. Suddenly, it came to me that the swimsuit was in the computer room, where I had left it the night before. I had forgotten entirely I placed my new swimsuit on the table adjacent to the computer. I could not wait to wear it. I headed to the computer room. There was no swimsuit, but the package the suit came in. Very disturbed, I yell to Esscence "have you seen my Louis Vuitton swimsuit? The package is here, but the swimsuit is not in it."

"No, mommy." "It should be there cause it was only me, you, and Mama. "I know, but it's not, so call her and ask if she moved it.

The following day after continuously going back and forth between Esscence and Mama, we finally received a call from Esscence's friend, Erika, who stated, "please don't say I told you, but she does have your mom's swimsuit cause Mama hid it under my bed. It's an expensive swimsuit, right?"

"Aaah!" yelled Esscence.

"Mommy, she has your swimsuit. She was trying to hide it to sell."

"Who, Esscence?"

"Mama." "She hid it under my friend's bed. She lives around the corner. I'm going to get it."

We arrived at Erika's house. I told Esscence not to go into the house in fear that Mama would find out that Erika ratted her out. Erika came out and said that the bathing suit was at her home with Mama. But when Mama found out that we were coming, she hid the swimsuit underneath her bed. Mama came out of the house, and I immediately approach her, asking why she stole my swimsuit when I always gave her what she wanted. After 20 minutes of talking back and forth, threatening to call the police, the swimsuit suddenly appears next to a garbage can outside Erika's house. Pissed and outraged, I express some very disrespectful words. I yelled at Esscence, "I told you, it was nothing but grimy written all over them. Do not you ever bring her thieving two pairs of jeans-wearing ass back to my house!

FULL FLETCH DRAMA

Now begins the drama with these females and this so-called man she so much loves. My daughter Chavon, Esscence, and I decided that we would go to the New York System in Olneyville to get some hot wieners. I pulled up to the establishment. Look who is there! Smurf with another female! I begin my speech, "Esscence, let it go." "I told you, he is not going to change." "You should just move on, please!" Out the car, she goes!

"Smurf, this is what we are doing?" Esscence sees the girl standing in the distance next to their car. She sees Esscence and begins to march toward her and Smurf.

"Who is she?" the girl said to Smurf as she walks towards them.

Chavon and I got out of the car to intervene. Grabbing Esscence and warning the female to keep it zipped. Esscence very troubled, I quickly removed her from the female's face that Smurf got caught cheating.

I began yelling, "You're a fucking disgrace and monster." As I escorted her back to the vehicle and started driving away. I calmly reminded Esscence that she was such a beautiful young lady with a child, so this was unnecessary to keep feuding with females over him.

A knock came on my door a few days later. It was Esscence.

"Mommy, you are not going to believe this." "You know the female I had the issue with the other day."

I became quiet while trying to recall. "Yes, I remember."

"She was with Smurf on Cranston Street." "She got dragged by a car because Smurf did something to a man over there."

I shake my head. "Esscence, are you not seeing the cycle." "This man is dangerous, and the devil must be his best friend." "Think about it." "Not too long ago, he was with his cousin, who is now deceased." "This woman gets dragged and almost dies." "You get in a fight with his baby's mother, kicking doors in because he goes back and forth with you and her." "Are you not getting it?" "I don't want you to think I am running your life Boops, but he is not good for you." "You are brilliant and beautiful." "Focus on you and Weezy." "Someone will come when the time is right."

A short time afterward, Smurf would finally be caught for his wrongdoings. With drug charges of possession, he was incarcerated.

THE NEW RELATIONSHIP

Esscence would move on and begin a relationship with another guy. Things went going well for months. I felt like I was breathing easier and sleeping well. Esscence was always an individual that could love you unconditionally. But do not step out of line because it was almost like she had a switch that flipped immediately if she felt disrespected.

Thursday evening, Chavon says mom, "I think Esscence is in Roger Williams Projects about to fight, cause she caught Man at a girl's house.

I let out a long exhale. I then dialed Esscence's phone number. By the second ring, a loud, angry HELLO was spoken on the other end.

"Esscence, what is going on?" "Tell me you are not fighting over a man."

"Mommy, I left. I am done with this!"

"You should have never let it begin Boops"! "Get home and leave these men alone if you can't handle the drama, they put you in."

One morning, I was up and getting ready for work. I heard a car door shut and glance out my bedroom window. I could not believe my eyes! The monster was out of jail! Esscence and him were walking up the stairs! I didn't know if I wanted to cry or just get the gun and lose everything!

As she was coming up the stairs, I stopped and said to her, "Essence, are you kidding me?"

"Mom, we are just hanging out."

Silence and just in shock. I thought he is back. Now the worrying begins once again.

We are back to hearing things from the street that he was involved in. I would have male family members approaching me, saying that they wanted to intervene because there was chatter on the street saying that Esscence was being manipulated and abused by him. Daily, I would try to get her to just fess up to the abuse, but there was always consistent denial.

NEW AIR

Chavon's two sisters and her father relocated to North Carolina. To my surprise, Esscence was ready to try a different environment to get away and smell the fresh air. All packed and ready, she was leaving. Dwayne would stay behind with his father to visit for two weeks to see if she wanted to move there. Every day, I would get a call. I could hear the smiles through the phone. Every night, I was begging God to put it on her heart to want to stay.

The weekend came, and I wanted to spend time with my grandson, so I go over to his grandmother's house on his father's side to pick him up. My family knows that I was big on school, so I said, "Weezy, nanny needs to see how you are doing with your homework."

He gives me a strange look then says, "Nannie Pie, I asked my daddy's girlfriend to help me, but she yelled and locked me in the room." I paused and started gathering my thoughts. "She did what?" "Did you tell anyone at your dad's this?" I asked while grabbing for the ringing phone. It was his father's grandmother. I immediately began questioning his grandmother about the girlfriend while sweat started running down my armpits. The grandmother explained she would find out and call me back. The grandmother called me back with a very disturbing response. That Dwayne did not do his homework, so she decided to lock him in the bedroom until he was done. After a brief silence, I tell the grandmother that I am on my way.

After I quickly hang up the phone, I get return phone calls pleading for me not to come there because she had left to go home. "Well, I will still be there." Quickly informing Chavon of the situation, we head to the grandmother's house. After a conversation with other family members and confirming what happened, I was off to find her. To this very day, no one believes that this now 5-year-old child had given us directions from one side of town to directly in front of her house. None of the family members were willing to provide information on her location, knowing the state of mind Chavon and I was in.

We pulled up to the front of the house. At the same time, we see a car pull into the driveway. Dwayne's father immediately exits the car and walks to the passenger side. Chavon looked at me and said, "Mom, I got this." She gets out of the car and proceeds to the vehicle, where two girls sit and say, "Which one of you is Bethany?" Neither one was willing to claim the name. Saying neither one was Bethany. Dad exits the side door and heads to the car with a distraught look, saying it is not her. A few more exchanges of words, and Chavon comes to the car asking her nephew, "Weezy, is that her in the car with your dad?" He nodded yes. A quick thought of "don't" pops into my head. The car pulls off, and we immediately follow the car, but the car picks up speed and rushes off. I fall back and head to the police station to file a report. The police are resistant to take a report because we are the grandmother and sister to the minor. They took the statement but explained that when Esscence returned, she would have to be the one to pursue the case.

Still truly angry, I did not call North Carolina to inform Esscence. She would have been on the next flight home. The following week, Esscence would return, and dreadfully, I would explain why I would keep Weezy and not return him to his father. About an hour after Esscence finished unpacking and telling us how her time was in North Carolina, she said she needed to go and pick up her son's things and follow-up with the police report. Knowing how Esscence's temper and mouth were, I said that I would take her. We arrive at Dwayne's great-grandmother's house. I explained to Esscence to be calm, get his things, and that is it. She says, mom, I am doing it the right way! We exit the car, and oh my, Weezy's father and the girlfriend are at the house. I quickly move closer to Esscence and follow her every footstep. In a loud voice, we hear, "don't even come in here talking shit, Esscence." "I already took care of it!" yelled Dwayne's father. Esscence looks to her left and notices that the girlfriend is in the kitchen. Esscence runs into the kitchen and yells, "Did you lock my son in the room?"

The girlfriend yells," yes, but you better not." Before she could get the rest of her sentence out, there was one punch, then another, and another. She starts screaming, "I am pregnant, and you are going to jail!" Before I can get Esscence out of the kitchen, Dwayne's dad begins punching Esscence and backing her into a corner. I immediately lost it, hitting the father until he backed off her. Emotions were out of control. We are now both taking turns punching and screaming at him, "Why are you so mad at us? You should have been angry at her and protecting your son!

Esscence would decide not to move to North Carolina. Between the hot air and the slow southern culture, she was not interested. I tried to persuade her to go back, saying that the 2-week visit was not enough time to decide. Also, explaining that North Carolina would be a better environment for Weezy, especially after the girlfriend fiasco.

THE BEGINNING OF THE END

Finally, the weekend was here. I would get off work and venture out to Club 650. This would be my time to wind down and relax. Moments after entering the club, I was approached by a stranger saying that Ari told her that either Todd or Esscence had fired a gun into a crowd to scare the group away because they were going to fight Esscence. The woman then said, "It was probably Esscence cause her boyfriend loves to use guns." I found this weird conversation because Esscence, Todd, or I went out that Friday night. Everyone was home.

The following week, I returned to Club 650. Ari, who was spreading the rumors, walks into the club. I immediately addressed her. I felt suspicious that this led to an organized plot against Smurf because I knew some people had deep beef with him.

The following morning, I heard a knock on the door. It was Boops. "Mom, can I ask you something?"

"Well, last night, Smurf was at a club, and someone shot up his car." "He did not get hit, but they wanted him, bad mommy, cause they said there were over 16 rounds in the car." "Do you think if he had been the one shot at the club last night, he would change his life and maybe love me?"

At that point, I could no longer sugarcoat my feelings. I responded NO!! "He will never love you, Esscence. He hits you, cheats on you, and is always getting someone hurt. He won't!"

"Sorry!" She begins to utter, "I am done this time, mommy, cause that could have been me in that car last night."

I quickly respond," That is all that I have been trying to tell you, Boops. I have heard stories with nothing but tragedy with him. Weezy should be your focus right now. "

"Okay, mommy, love you. I promise I am done."

November 3rd, Boops comes to the door. "Mommy, I got my apartment." "I can move in on the 15th." "OG, I am souped!"

At that moment, I tried to show excitement in her presence, but as soon as she stepped out of the room, I immediately began to cry and shake my head. Todd, with a weird look on his face, said, "What is wrong? Why are you crying? She must live, Diana. She is not a baby anymore."

"He is going to ruin her life, and I can't stop it." Now I cannot see what is going on with her out of the house! I do not want her and my grandson alone with that bastard at all. She is working, just got her car, and is doing well. Fuuuuuck!!!!"

November 15th comes; Esscence is looking upset and bothered.

"Boops, what is wrong?"

"Smurf told me that he would give me the money to move into my apartment tomorrow cause I let him use it." "Now he doesn't have it." After an exceptionally long pause, upset but calm, saying, "Boops, I am not sure why you would give him money, but you need to make sure you get it back and not let it happen again. He should be providing for you." "Please, can I ask why you would still be involved with him?"

"I know, mommy, but he promised to give it back!"

In a sarcastic tone, I respond with, "Okay, Boops!" "How much do you need to move in? I will give it to you." "Get what you gave him to me and leave him alone!"

"Thank you, mommy. I love you."

She now has the keys to her new apartment. After work, I figured I would go, see her new house, and help her get things moved in. Two days later, I picked her up to go to the market to get food and household items. She reached into her purse and said, "thank you so much for the money, mommy. I appreciate it." It was her paycheck from work. Feeling anger but proud, I handed her the check back and said, get what you and Weezy need. Make sure you use it for what it is for. She hugs me and almost releases tears on my shoulder but being Boopsie; she holds it in. Shopping we go!

Now four days later, I get a phone call from Chavon. "Mommy, I am about to go over and smash on Smurf!"

"What is wrong?" "Don't tell Ess, but he took her house keys and threw them somewhere, and she can't get in her house." "She is pissed because it is only her fourth day in her new apartment, and he is doing this."

After a long silence, I responded that I had enough of this shit. I will see you in a bit after I get out of work. Later that night, when I got home, Esscence was waiting on me at the house. She told me what had transpired. Without control of my thoughts, I told her I had enough with the shit he is doing to her. You need to get rid of his ass before I end up in jail! I know you don't want me to go to jail?"

"I know, mommy." "I am done." I told him he couldn't stay with me and that I was done with him." "That is why he took my keys and threw them. Now I have to pay to get into my apartment."

Shaking my head and muttering this bastard under my breath, I get up to get ready to take her to her apartment. All along, I was glad that Weezy was not yet staying there and was with his father.

Sunday came, and it was my typical day when I would cook for the brats. The call I knew would usually go by 3 in the afternoon. It was Boops. "Mommy, is the food done yet?"

"No, it is not, maybe in about an hour or so.

"Oh my gosh, mommy, I am starving!"

"You are always starving skinny. Just come in about an hour."

"Sigh! Okay, see you then.

About two hours later, I heard the 105-pound child sounding like she weighed like a 300-pound man coming up the stairs.

"Mommy, my food better be ready."

"It's done cry-baby. After 10 minutes of aggravating Chavon, which is her usual routine, she trots back down the stairs and right into the kitchen.

After dinner, I said to her, "if you are ready, Boops, I can bring you home, so you don't have to take the bus with all the food. I know you have to wait for you downstairs!"

A low giggle, "No, that is okay, I have a ride."

With a look of dismay and concern, I asked, "who was coming to pick her up?"

"China."

"What?" "Why is he coming to pick you up Ess?" He and his girl argued, and he asked if he could stay for the night."

Very mad with visible steam coming out my ears, I said, "Ess, didn't you just tell me that you were done with his brother, Smurf, and staying away from him?" "So why are you talking to his brother?"

"I am mommy. He is not there!"

"Esscence, I am not going to give you a speech, but please just leave him alone. "You just told me that you were done and didn't want to be around him because his car was just shot up a week ago, right?"

"Yes, mommy, I am not with him. I learned my lesson that he is not good for me."

Upset and worried, I responded with "okay, Ess." "Do the right thing, please." "You have Weezy." "Just know that you will be blessed with someone who will love you like the Queen you are." "I always tell you are okay!"

"I know, mommy." "I will call you as soon as I get home."

The phone rings about half an hour later.

"Mommy, I am home and will call you in the morning." Do you think you can make me one of those tuna sandwiches you get at work?"

"Yes, greedy." "Come down to my job at twelve." 'See you then." Love you, Boops."

"Love you too, mommy."

Monday at 9:15 am, I received my normal morning call from Ess.

"Mommy, what are you doing?"

"Ummmm, working!"

"What eva big head." "Don't forget my sandwich and something to drink too." "See you then."

At 12:05, she comes to my job to grab her tuna sandwich and drink. "Love you, mommy." "Todd is bringing me to the house to get some more of Weezy's and my stuff.

"Ok, I will be over after I get out."

It is now 5:00 pm, and Todd is outside, ready to go to Essence's house. We arrive at her home. It looked much better than when she moved in a couple of days ago. It was coming along lovely.

Esscence was always that spoiled brat who I could never even dream of saying no to. "What else do you need?"

"Just my kitchen and bathroom stuff."

"Put something on, and let's go." All smiles as we are off to Walmart. After two hours of shopping, we head back to her house, and I help her Walmart bags into her apartment.

"Okay skinny." "I will call you later." Have a good night, and love you."

For the rest of the week, I get my normal early morning call from Esscence.

The Saturday before Thanksgiving, my niece, Shanda, phones and says, "Aunty Diana, Candy is coming down with the kids for Thanksgiving." "I want everyone to come to my house this year."

Happy and elated, "I love you, Shanda girl. "I can't wait to come and slam on your good ole food!" "What do you need me to bring?

"Aunty, just grab something to drink." I immediately dial the phone to call Boops to tell her that we will be spending Thanksgiving with Shanda. I know Esscence will be happy because she was supposed to cook Thanksgiving at her new house, but she did not have everything together, being that she had just moved in on the 17th.

"Oh yup, can't wait, mommy!" "What are you doing with your big head? "Shut up, Boops." "What are you doing?"

"I am getting ready to hop on the bus to go and chill with Aunty Barbara at Meisha's house." "I will call you when I get there."

"Ok, love you."

THANKSGIVING DAY

The Last Goodbye

Finally, Thanksgiving Day was here. The phone rings around 11 am. It was Esscence.

"Mommy, are we still going to Cousin Shanda's, right?"

"Yes, so be ready by 4."

When we arrived at my niece's house, they were family members we had not seen in a while. One of those members was Candance. She was there with our two cousins. Her mother, Debra, was also in attendance, which had traveled up from Atlanta. We were also surprised to see that Ebony, a family friend we had not seen in about five years.

After prayer, dinner, and talks of long-lost memories, it was time for the battle of the "Christal Gals." The night would not have been thoroughly enjoyed if we did not have our ritual dance-off. Chavon, Esscence, and Shyanne would be the ones to set-it-off! This battle would go on for almost 30 minutes. In addition to the dance-off, we played spades and continued to eat Thanksgiving dinner and dessert. We were all boozed up and full of Thanksgiving food. By the end of the night, we were utterly exhausted.

A bizarre thing came about as Shanda chimed, "it's picture time." "You know we gotta have those pics."

We all began to gather in her living room area, where all the little ones watched TV. Esscence comes over and says with a very playful and joyous smile, "I am going to sit on my mommy's lap for this picture, so you need to give Mya to someone else, mommy."

I looked at her and said, "Boops, you are not sitting on my lap with your skinny self. "Your bones are going to hurt my leg."

"Yes, I am," Esscence said with a cheerful look on her face. Finally, she says, gotcha, big head; I do not want to sit on your lap. I look around, and she is sitting on the floor in front of the entire family, ready for the picture to be taken. I am sitting still, a little taken back. I know how much my baby loves me, but she was particularly clingy with a weird sort of glow that I never saw before.

Click after click; we took many different pictures. Before we decide to part ways, she comes over and says, "Mommy, you're the best." "I love you."

I begin to say to God; my baby is growing up. I think she has realized that she is ready to move on and get her life right and away from that jerk. I grab my things, kissing and hugging everyone and telling Shanda how much fun we had.

She says, "hey y'all, how about we do this again tomorrow since it is Friday?" "We can spend more time with Candy."

We all agreed and were parting ways when Esscence says, "Mommy, can you and Uncle Todd take me home?"

"I was already planning on it cause you seem a little tipsy."

"Shut up, big head." "Let's go!"

We had so many people to drop off; my little skinny Minnie would have to sit on her mommy's lap after all. We arrived at her house, and I said, "are you sure you don't want to come to stay at the house instead of staying home by yourself."

"No, mommy." "I am going to turn on the tv and knock out." "Okay, Boops, love you." "See you for round two tomorrow. "

There would be no round two! The following morning was strange because I did not get my regular morning call from Esscence. I called her, and the phone went to voicemail. I waited a while longer and called again. Once again, it went to voicemail. With a little worry, I said, "Todd, I have not heard from Boops, and I want to go check on her."

As I was getting ready to go shower to get dressed, the phone rings. It is Boops.

"Where are you, and why didn't you call me this morning? "

"My bad, big head." "I left my charger at Meisha's house." "I am back over here having a couple of drinks with Aunty Barbara."

I said to Esscence, "I was wondering if you all were still going to Shanda's house."

There was a pause from Esscence. Then she said, "I kinda don't feel like going." "I want to just chill with Cousin Shy and Aunty Barbara."

"Ok. I will call Shanda and tell her we will come chill with her and Candy tomorrow.

"Ok."

"Tell Aunty and the girls I love them."

"Ok, call you later. Love you."

Leaning over to Todd, I say, "Well, I guess we'll just relax, listen to some music and watch movies because they are going to stay in tonight."

Family Picture on Thanksgiving Day

THE LOUD BANG

After watching tv, I finally knock out around 1:45 in the early morning. At 2:42 am, I hear a loud bang. Bang! Bang! I jumped up and say to Todd, "Who the hell is kicking on the door like that?" "I bet that is Boopsie!" I go downstairs and peek out of my front door window.

It is my niece, Shyanne.

"Aunty, please hurry up." "We have to get to the hospital!

"What's wrong, Shy?"

"Aunty, it is Esscence." "She was in a car accident and shot!"

"What the fuck do you mean?" "OMG!" "What are you saying, Shy?"

"Aunty, please just get to the hospital."

I jetted back up the stairs, puzzled and breathless. "Todd, please get up. "Shy is at the door." "She said Ess was shot and was in an accident."

"Yoooo!" "Come on!" "What the fuck you mean?"

On my way past Chavon's bedroom door, she screams, "Mommy, what is going on?" "Did you say my sister was in an accident and shot?" "No, mommy, please, what is going on?"

Down the stairs, out the door, and in the car with my niece Shyanne and her friend.

"Shy." I said, "Please tell me Ess is alive."

"Yes, Aunty." "We need to get there."

We arrived at the hospital. I saw so many people in the waiting area. Some people were crying. Some people had weird looks on their faces. Others talked with anxiety and worry.

"I need to see my daughter Esscence," I said to the nurse at the registration desk.

"Ma'am, what is your name?"

"It does not matter." "I need to see my daughter."

For some strange reason, no Smurf in my view! Moments went by. I was walking and panting. Where is my daughter? I thought.

"Can someone please get the doctor?" "I am getting ready to go to the back room."

A quick turnaround, and here comes Smurf through the door.

"Smurf, what happened to Boops?" I ask again. "Smurf, what happened to Boops?"

Smurf stares for a moment, then he responds, "I think she was shot in the neck."

"Is she okay, Smurf?"

"I think so." "Umm, I don't know."

"What the fuck do you mean you don't know Smurf?" "My baby better be okay." "Where is the doctor?"

"Ma'am, give us a minute, and we will get the doctor."

"No." "Why the fuck can't I see my baby?" "Where is she?" "Is she alive?"

SHE'S GONE

The doctor finally comes out and calmly says, "Ma'am, follow me, please!"

"Where is my baby?"

We head toward a quiet room. "OMG!" I said, screaming and crying. "OMG." "Please don't bring me to that fucking room. "Where is my baby?" "Bring me to my baby right now, please!" "Lord, please, don't let my baby be gone!" "Lord, why would you do this to me? "Where is my baby?"

I suddenly feel my heart pounding and my legs growing weak. I hear the nurse ask me, "Ma'am, can you tell me if your daughter has a tattoo with your name?"

"Noooo!" "God, please bring my baby back." "Lord, why?" "Why is she asking me this question, Todd?"

Todd immediately becomes outraged, "Where the fuck in Smurf?"

"Sir, where are you going?" asked the nurse.

"Where the fuck is Smurf?" He begins running through the hospital halls yelling for Smurf. I hear a loud commotion and officers running to the front of the hospital.

" OMG!" "What is going on?" "Where is my baby?" "If my baby is gone, I will kill him!" "I am going to kill him!"

The nurse and the other doctors came rushing in and began giving me oxygen due to a quick collapse that I had suffered. Suddenly, I was awake. The nurse says, "I am sorry, ma'am." "We tried everything we could to save her." "We went to the extent of cracking open her chest, ma'am." "She fought very hard to stay with us but couldn't hang on."

Sitting in a blank stare, all I could hear was that she was gone, over and over and over again—scream after scream, and another long look. The officers brought Todd back into the room.

"Please don't leave this room, sir. "Unfortunately, we will have to arrest you if you try to assault him again."

"Are you fucking serious?" Todd yells. "He let my daughter get shot, and you want to arrest me!" "I don't give a fuck, arrest me!" "I am going to fucking kill him!"

Todd's cell phone rings and rings; he finally picks it up.

"Where is my sister? The voice on the phone asks. "What happened to Ess?" "Please come get me, Todd."

After a long pause, Todd said, "she didn't make it." Chavon starts screaming through the phone. Todd's cell phone hangs up on her.

I say to Todd, "Someone needs to go get her." "Please, someone, go get her with all the kids."

"Ma'am, we have to make sure you are okay." The nurse began to say. "Can we please check you out again?" "You fainted, and we need to make sure you are okay to leave."

"No, I am fine." "I need to find out who shot my fucking daughter cause I am going to jail!"

A very hurt look appears on the nurse's face. "Ma'am, I need to tell you something." "It was disturbing." "The man that brought your daughter in from the accident put her on a chair and said he had to leave because he left his shoe at the scene." "He left the hospital."

"Are you fucking kidding me?" "What guy?"

"The guy your husband was trying to fight."

An immediate change in demeanor, I go on to say, "I am going to kill him, so can you please tell my kids I love them, and I am sorry?" "He put my fucking baby down on a bench to die alone!" "He is dead." "Let me out of this room." "Please move." "I don't want to hurt you!"

"No, ma'am." "Someone, please get an officer to watch the guy in the ER." "The parents are not in their right state of mind, and I believe I will do him harm." "Please get the officers now!"

A significant presence of officers was now in the room. They began to say, "We know this hard." "We are sorry, but you have to leave the hospital." While being escorted out of the hospital, I run into Smurf. "Smurf, tell me who killed my baby!" "Smurf, you better tell me, or you are going to be dead next."

"I can't say right now."

"You fucking bastard." "You better give me the names, or I promise you, you are dead!"

A woman's quiet and timid voice, "Ma'am, please don't threaten anyone." "I understand your pain."

"Shut the fuck up." "You don't know fucking no my pain." "Are you fucking kidding me?" "Smurf, you will die if you don't give me those fucking names!"

As Todd and I were escorted to a bench outside of the hospital, Smurf begins to yell, "I am fucking killing them, I promise you!" as he is walking down the hospital sidewalk to leave.

I turned to him and responded, "You better or you will not live Smurf." "I promise you." "Give me the names!"

I began to battle with different emotions. Each one of these emotions was giving me crazy thoughts. I told myself there were many officers standing around with their shiny guns. I should grab one and shoot this piece of shit! I started to ramble, "He laid my baby on a bench cause he left his fucking shoe"! My mind said, Diana, he must die! This played over and over. But then something says, you must live for Weezy and the other children!

Calls on top of calls came pouring in. I did not feel like answering. I finally spoke to my son Lamar, and the phone drops the call. There was no answer as I tried to call back. We have to get the kids and check on Chavon.

We get home. With a look of disbelief, pain, and grief, Chavon begins screaming, crying, and pacing the floor. "Mommy, where is my sister?" "Mommy, go get my sister." The kids were in dismay and began to cry. Weezy looks up, goes, and sits on the bed with his head down. He would not speak. I immediately call his father with the bad news asking him to please come and get Weezy while we try and get ourselves together. It was now time to break the bad news to her older sister Keyonna, who was living in Woonsocket at the time. She did not have a phone, so we drove to Woonsocket to tell her that Esscence has passed. We arrive at her apartment to tell Keyonna, and she drops to the floor immediately. Screaming and asking us to please tell her it is a dream. After moments of consoling, we prepare to head back to Providence to begin this emotional rollercoaster.

PROVIDENCE, R.I. — The woman shot to death while driving on Broad Street early Saturday has been identified as 21-year-old **Esscence T. Christal, of Providence.**

Christal, a young mother from Indiana Avenue, was driving Arney Hepburn, 27, and James "Smurf" Perkins, 28, at around 1:45 a.m. when they noticed a dark four-door vehicle following them, according to police.

The vehicle pulled along the passenger side of their car, and someone opened fire. As the gunman's car drove off, Christal's vehicle smashed into a tree and flipped over.

A passerby brought Christal and Perkins to Rhode Island Hospital, where the young woman died. **Perkins, who was the front-seat passenger, was treated for injuries and released.**

THE REVEAL

Two days later, after contemplating washing down all 40 sleeping pills, the doctor had prescribed me, the phone rings. I cannot believe the voice I hear on the other end. It is Smurf!

"Can I please come and talk to you about what happened?"

I immediately interrupted and asked, "Who did it?"

"I also need to be at the funeral." "I have to say goodbye to Ess."

A quick breath, "You must be fucking kidding me." "You want to call me two days later to talk."

"Yes, please, I will tell you everything."

"Let me just ask you something." "Did you place my baby on a bench to go get your shoe?"

"I can explain." "I had some things I had to go do!"

"You left Smurf?"

Now my mind was racing so badly. I began to get an instant headache. "You're telling me that you know who it is but wouldn't tell the police?" "Yes, please just let me come there."

"Yes, you can come over." Please pray you can leave."

"I don't want any problems. I just want to tell you what happened, please."

"You need to cover over and tell us what happened." After that, I hung up the phone on Smurf. I went upstairs to explain to Todd that Smurf wanted to talk and tell us who shot Esscence.

"Tell him to come." "Are you going to be able to do this, Diana?" Todd asked.

"I need to know who I am going to kill."

Smurf arrives. It is dark and cold outside. I said to come in. As I was closing the door, I looked out and saw someone waiting in the car. I thought that whoever was in the car would not save him if I decided to take his life in my house.

"Come upstairs where we can talk privately."

"I don't trust going upstairs."

"If I wanted to kill you, you would have been dead the moment you stepped in the door."

He slowly approaches the stairs looking over his shoulder. Proceeding to my room upstairs, Chavon comes out of her bedroom screaming, "You fucking got my sister killed!" "Why the fuck you here?"

"Hold on, Chavon!" "We are going to talk about what happened to Esscence."

"Fuck him, mommy!" "Just kill him now."

He reaches toward his pocket. "Smurf don't be reaching for your fucking pocket," Todd says.

"Well, she is saying to kill me."

"What the fuck is in your pocket?"

"I brought my knife. Fuck that."

"Well, I said talk." "Then you can get the fuck out and go on with your life," I said.

About 4 minutes into the conversation, he begins speaking the names; Taja, Juke, Nell, and Scoob are in one car.

"Are you fucking kidding me, Smurf?" In a state of shock, I shouted, "That is her fucking brother's family!" I was very distraught and feeling incredibly sick. I said, "Who the fuck is Taja, Smurf?"

"He was in the vehicle with two other people that I could not see." "Also, we already had beef because of my cousin Lennie!"

I begin shouting and hitting the door. "I told her to stay away from you." "You knew they were after you, Smurf!" "The day that you and homeboy exchanged words, both of you supposedly squashed it because his girlfriend and Esscence lived right across from each other." "I knew something was going to happen"!

"Well, he is the one who sent them after me." "All this shit goes back to the crazy shit Big Honda was doing to my boys, period!"

"So, was dating Esscence a payback, Smurf?" "C'mon now"! "Why did you put her in the car?" "They said she didn't want to go!"

There was a pause without a response.

"What are you going to do about this Smurf"? "What are you going to do"?

"The police want me to testify and move out of state." "I can't do that!" "I can't be a snitch." "I have to take care of it myself!"

"So, you are not going to tell?"

"I already told the police that I would not testify."

"Okay, well, I pray that you continue to live a nice and safe life, but I can't be the one to promise you that."

"Are you threatening me after I told you what happened?"

"No way." "I promise you that I will pray that you make it through to see your kids grow up; cause Weezy won't see his mom."

"Well, I am out of here cause that's fucked up." "I gave you the info, and you still want to threaten me."

"I never liked you, Smurf." "I wanted to kill you the day you put your hands on my baby, and now I have even more of a reason to do it!"

"Okay, I guess it's an issue with us too."

"No guessing, there is an issue!"

"So, I can't even go to the funeral to say my goodbye?"

"Fuck no." "She is dead because of you. "You don't deserve to say goodbye." "You refuse to do the right thing and lock them motherfuckers under the jail." "Fuck no, bye!"

"What about my kids?"

"What about her son?" "You knew what kind of beef you had, and you still chose to put her in the situation to get her shot!" "How are you living right now?" "How long do you think you will live?" "You told me who they are?" "Do you think I am going to stay quiet?"

"I got this!" Smurf replied.

"You don't have shit!" "You need to call the police and testify because you would be lucky to even live yourself!"

 "Well, that's a chance I have to take."

The day after Esscence was shot and killed, people talked and repeated the names that Smurf had given to us. They kept stating that Esscence would allegedly die at the hands of her own brother's family! Still devastated by her death, I contemplated approaching everyone. I was beginning to get angrier, thinking, why would I not be able to do the unthinkable and pull the trigger myself!

The following day after that conversation with Smurf, the death became more hurtful and grievous. A knock on the door, and it was a face that was very shocking to see. It was Smurf's brother's girlfriend. I immediately give Chavon a look of "what the fuck."

"Well, I just came to say I am sorry and also tell you that Esscence wasn't herself lately." "The last night before it happened, she came by the house and was nervous."

Interrupting her, I said, "What?" "What do you mean?"

"She was just acting weird and not herself."

Still confused, I asked again, "What do you mean?"

"I don't know, just nervous."

"Well, I don't understand what you are saying." I got frustrated and left the room. Another knock on the door was another person, who makes me cringe.

"Yo, Chavon!" Jess said with a deep and sarcastic tone.

"Yo, I can't believe this shit." "I heard they used those big-ass guns to shoot Ess for real. Sorry to say it like that, but they did."

"What the fuck!" "Why would you think we want to fucking hear that shit right now?" I ask. "Who the fuck is saying that?"

"I just heard that shit."

"Again, from who?"

Chavon and Jess continue to ignore me and not answer. At this moment, my only thought was to shoot the entire city up until I couldn't anymore. Todd had begun to see the anger in me growing, so he quickly grabs me and says, "you need just to go lay down." "No more people."

That was not happening because there were more phone calls and visits.

Later that night, after people began to leave, I heard a knock on the door. It was a neighbor with a dish. With a story to share that would make me just want to die.

"I apologize, but I knew something had happened when I saw all these people." "Was it your daughter?"

Puzzled, I said, "Yes." "How did you know?"

"I am asking because I feel bad." "A few nights ago, she was sitting in the car with that guy she is always with. "He was hitting, yelling, and being aggressive to her. She was telling him that she couldn't be with him because her mother said he had people trying to kill him and she needed to stay away." "The last straw for me was when I heard her scream and say don't. Do not burn me with that cigarette lighter. I jumped up out of my chair on the porch and said I would call the cops. He immediately sped off with her in the car." My heart felt like it stopped. I could not take any more of the conversation and just walked away.

FUNERAL

On the day of the funeral, a big black limousine pulled up in front of the house. I felt weak and was trying to muster up the strength to say goodbye to my Boopsie. I will probably end up being buried.

After time passes, I finally get the courage to go and say my final goodbye. I enter the funeral home, and suddenly, I become short of breath. Todd reaches out to me to hold my hand, trying to guide me to her shiny pink coffin. "No, I can't do this!" I cried. Approaching the coffin, I see her! My Boopsie in that coffin! No life and gone! Why, Why, Why! Lord, what did I do? I said over and over and over.

People came in and talked to me. I blocked out everything except for the words "sorry for your loss." I heard it over and repeatedly. Then suddenly, I looked up and saw the fire in the eyes of Dwayne's father and my son, Lamar. I jumped up to see what was causing these fierce looks, and in comes Smurf with his mother and brother. The funeral home erupted in chaos, yelling, hitting, and police flooding into the parlor! Who would have ever imagined witnessing this kind of drama at a funeral? Screaming and crying, I ask him, why did he come? The funeral director and his staff got the parlor back in order, but they cut the service short with no more viewings! My heart was crushed because now I do not even finish my baby's homegoing service properly.

As time passes, we begin to try and move on in life. The chatter, looks, anger, and shady actions start. Esscence's death would begin to bring so much to the light. People would be conversing with Chavon or me and say, I know who did it, but I wouldn't know anything! We would be in stores, and friends who laughed and joked with us before her killing, would suddenly turn their heads and walk in another direction. At the same time, others would just give us a weird stare and continues without conversation. Nothing but lies and deceit would continue to follow. I recall one phone conversation that would leave me waking up for many nights crying, balled up into a knot, and thinking constantly, what kind of mother are you to just lay here sobbing instead of making them pay? The family member called and said, "I don't want to ask you this question, but how many times was Esscence shot?" I was holding the phone trembling and immediately respond, "What?" "Why?"

I am asking for a reason. "Was she shot in a particular part of her body?"

"Why are you even asking me this?' "What the fuck is going on?" Her response was, "because I would like to know how an individual would know that type of information. She then asked me if Esscence was shot in a particular place on her body. (Please note that the author chooses not to share that information with the public.)

I replied, "Yes."

"It's exactly what I thought," she said. "He should have never known this information unless he was involved."

At this point, I thought to myself, "there is no trust, love, or loyalty for anyone!"

We decided to go to the bar I frequented before Essence's death. After many condolences and conversations, an acquaintance enters the bar and comes over to the table where we were seated.

They asked, "Can you please come to the back with me?" "I have something important to tell you."

I proceeded to the back, wondering what this conversation could be about. She tells me to come into the bathroom. Before I could completely enter, she lets out a loud burst of tears.

"What is wrong?"

"I can't take it anymore."

"What?"

"I can't believe they killed her."

For a moment, I was shocked, then mixed with a whole lot of emotions. "Who?" "Who are you talking about?"

She offers up names, and I immediately lose my composure and begin to tear up. "Why are you saying this?" "I asked because I know this is individual." "They are blood family to the alleged perpetrators."

"I don't fucking care." "I loved Esscence." "She didn't deserve that." He should be the one gone!"

Still not able to believe her words, I just held the acquaintance and said, "I knew it was true, but nothing would be done about this." "Smurf is not going to speak up, so there is nothing I can do."

She grabbed me again said that she was sorry. I knew it was genuine and sincere by the look in her eyes. After composing ourselves, we hugged and said that we love each other. What the monster had said was confirmed. I returned to the table where Todd and Chavon were sitting.

"Mommy, what happened," Chavon asked. With a head shake and tears rolling down my eyes, I explained what happened in the bathroom.

"I can't believe it's true." "Mommy, call the police.

"They won't be able to do anything because there is no way in hell. They will repeat what was said."

"Fuck that!" 'They are not going to walk away from killing my sister."

"I know Chavon!" "I don't know how much longer I can walk around and not get justice."

That very conversation brought me back to a situation that transpired a few months before she was murdered. I was sitting outside of a house we would frequent to chill and drink. A car pulls up with two males. I recognize one guy because he grew up with my son and was like family. Excuse me, are you Lamar's mom. A quick giggle, "you know who I am." "I also knew about the drama he was having with Essence's boyfriend."

"Well, can you tell Esscence to stay out of the car with Smurf cause we are going to get him?"

Shaking my head as the car pulls away, I immediately call Esscence to relay the message. I told you he is trouble, and you need to stay away from him. In very soft-spoken words, Esscence had said, "Okay, mommy." "I know things are not good with him." "I will stay away!"

Chavon said, "Mommy, I know you are going to be mad probably, but Esscence told me that one day she and Smurf were coming down the street. And that same person jumped out and tried to stab Smurf.

One of the worst interactions and disbelief was when I was walking into a local Walmart. I saw a close family member, and the individual lowered their head and pretended not to see me.

"What the fuck is that all about?" I said to myself. I was even more pissed cause this individual did not even attend my baby's funeral! What was being hidden? Why was I avoided? As time went on, this encounter would occupy my mind so much that I began to lose faith and trust in everyone and everything.

Just when I thought I had heard and seen enough. About a year or so later, I was pulling up to my house. I had not seen the neighbor in a while; he comes over and greets me with a hug and a very remorseful look. We continue chatting, and I finally asked where he had been? He quickly responds, locked up. He says that he was locked up with Homeboy, the other individual who was in the car with Ess and Smurf. He told me that he was messed up because she did not want to get into that car, and Smurf had forced her. He gave an account of how they were being chased, how Smurf heard the shots ringing out and began to lay his seat back as far as it could go instead of shielding Esscence.

I began to tremble and busted into uncontrollable tears. My neighbor then stated I am sorry, but I think you should know what is being said. He went on to say that her brother's family was responsible, but Homeboy could not testify because his mother is well known, and he will not put that on her. So angry and distraught, I immediately interrupt, saying, well, I guess Weezy not having a mother does not matter, huh. You know what; fuck this grimy ass city and everyone in it, I said as I walked away, with my neighbor stating he was sorry.

THE LEGACY BEGINS

As the time approached for the family and me to attend the Peace Rally, I began to panic. We arrived at Children's Family Service, where the nonviolence rally was being held. There were so many people in the parking lot that I began to panic because I had never been able to speak to many people. About 20 minutes into the event, Kobi approached the microphone and said, "Today, I have a mother who lost her daughter to gun violence and is here to share her story. Please welcome Diana Garlington."

Slowly I approached the microphone while my family holds a sign with a picture of Esscence on it with the words were written: "speak up." I nervously began to speak. As I shared my story, I noticed the crowd receiving my words with loud claps and shaking of heads in agreement with tears and smiles. This day would be the confirmation I had prayed so hard about. Esscence's legacy had to be carried on for justice and fight for other mothers and families to help stop these senseless acts of violence.

After the abundance of love given during my speech, Kobi would ask me to meet him for lunch to discuss ways to continue the fight. The following week, we met for lunch at a local restaurant called South Street Cafe. An enjoyable but serious conversation began, leading me to tear up. He said to me that it was time for me to start building Esscence's legacy instead of continuing to mourn. He felt that her legacy would be strong with me advocating. After that, we started to plan ways to build her legacy.

Before our departure, there it was, we would have a bowling fundraiser. We figured people loved to bowl and that this would also be a time for families to bond. "Bowl 4 Esscence" fundraiser was born. That was just the beginning of what would be done in her remembrance. We planned toy drives, rolling skating events, and an elegant meet and greet at one of our upscale Japanese restaurants named Oki's.

Peace Rally at Lockwood Plaza

SHE WASN'T THE ONE (POEM)

She wasn't the one. Didn't you notice it was her, when she took off down Broad Street and kept trying to run?

She wasn't the one. You chased her for 5 blocks with what I heard was with the big guns.

She wasn't the one. On that night just 3 hours earlier you could have taken her son.

She wasn't the one. She was 21 years old and her life had just begun.

She wasn't the one. You left her family heartbroken and stricken with grief.

She wasn't the one. Who came at you and brought you all this nonsense beef.

She wasn't the one. She watched you premeditate a scheme and drive around with 3 to 4 deep.

She wasn't the one. Who should have been put in that grave and now will forever sleep.

I wasn't the one you chose to end my life and shoot me from that car.

I wasn't the one now your day is coming because I know who you are…

HOMICIDE (POEM)

Life is a struggle and I am living proof. Cowards pulled the trigger and left me crying, dying, and looking for the crew.

He suddenly got quiet, but waits, wasn't you the target but refused to give justice to your so-called Boo?

But mommy I love him, when I got to the hospital, he was no longer in view. Smurf tell me you didn't lean your seat back, watched total strangers pull her out that car because there was no sign of a rescue, Nurse says I am sorry but the man that she adored went back to the scene because he lost his fucking shoe!!

Passenger in the back goes to jail and tells the whole story of how Esscence died. They both sang like birds to the ones on the inside. One comes out his neck but I know they know my mother, so I won't testify, but what about her mother and her only child? Yes, I get mad and I rant, but I lost my baby daughter, what do you expect me to do? They say karma made its rounds not one, not two. I can go on and on, but I would have to get very disrespectful. They took my baby girl while her murder gets to eat, sleep, and vibe. They continue taking bullets and repping these streets. Wake up little Providence. Do not get caught slipping or taking that ride, because you may be added to that number and labeled Unsolved Homicide!!!

KOBI DENNIS, COMMUNITY LEADER

After close to a year after Esscence was killed, I was asked to go to an event where there would be community leaders meeting to talk about curbing violence in our community. I attended a brunch where there would be individuals I have never either met, or laid eyes on. We sat and brainstormed while I was constantly consoled for the loss of Esscence. Finally, a man comes in and states that his name is Kobi Dennis, and one of the leaders of the community. After the brunch, he said, I am so sorry for the loss of your daughter, and I think you should consider coming to some of the meetings, I know it won't stop the pain, but I think you can heal by getting out in the community and helping others so they will not have to endure the same pain you did "No Disrespect" just saying you can make an impact sharing your story about your daughter. I am hosting an event next month in Lockwood Plaza and I would like you and your family to come. I will think about it and be in touch. When I got home, I explained to my family what was discussed, and they agreed that I should at least attend.

LOCK ARMS FOR PEACE

A Call for Unity and Peace

Our community had suffered violently throughout the years from gun violence.

Founded by Kobi Dennis and now coordinated by Diana; "Locking Arms for Peace" addresses the issue of gun violence within the community. Our mission is to honor those who lost their lives, call for unity amongst the people and facilitate peace throughout the neighborhoods.

"Locking Arms for Peace" has developed into activities based, mission driven, community event held once a month in Providence, Rhode Island and some surrounding cities. Activities such as face-painting, spoken word and t-shirt giveaways have been included in the event.

"Locking Arms for Peace" was featured on WPRI.com.

"Anti-violence advocates 'lock arms for peace' in Providence"
https://www.wpri.com/news/local-news/providence/anti-violence-advocates-lock-arms-for-peace-in-providence/

For more information, follow Author Diana Garlington on Facebook.

UNSOLVED MURDER VICTIMS LIST FOR THE CITY OF

PROVIDENCE (YR 2000- YR 2013)

April 16, 2000-Dennys A. Cabrera of Sackett Street. Witnesses said they saw Cabrera walking on near Sackett Street when he collapsed. Was stabbed in the torso. Stabbing

May 16, 2000-Hector Perez, 23, of Melrose Street. Perez was shot on Melrose Street and driven to Rhode Island Hospital by friends. Shooting

June 6, 2000-Jesus Caban, 38, of Prescott Street. Caban was shot and died at the scene. Shooting

July 14, 2000-John Hyman, 17, of Somerset Street. Witnesses said they heard ten-gun shots and police recovered five shell casings. Hyman died at Rhode Island Hospital. Shooting

August 3, 2000-Angel Cruz, 19, of Almy and Penn Street. Shot in the face. Found dead at the scene. Shooting

August 5, 2000-Kenneth Kilgore, 28, of Glimore Street. Kilgore was found in his car after being shot several times. He died at Rhode Island Hospital. A second victim was wounded but lived. Shooting

August 7, 2000-Benjamin DeWillis, 23, of Fremont Street Was shot in his head and died at Rhode Island Hospital. Shooting

August 8, 2000- Omar Gomez, 21, of Sumter Street. Gomez sustained numerous gunshot wounds and was pronounced dead at the scene. Shooting

Nov 23, 2000- Diogenes Ramos, 29, of Bridgham Street. Shot several times and pronounced dead at the scene. Shooting

Nov 25, 2000- Donnie Smith, 26, of Silver Spring Street. Was found on the ground with gunshot wounds. Pronounced dead at Rhode Island Hospital. Shooting

Dec 20, 2000- Eric Price, 32, of Erastus Street. Price was found dead at the scene. Another victim was wounded but survived. Shooting

Dec 22, 2000-Jay Robinson, 19, of Lockwood Street. Was found near a dumpster with a gunshot would. Pronounced dead at Rhode Island Hospital. Shooting

2000-Tyrone Collins, 18, of March Street was found dead at the scene with a gunshot wound. A second person was wounded, by survived. Shooting

April 10, 2001-Hani Zaki, 51, of Prospect Street. Well-known doctor was found dead in his East Side home. Shooting

July 4, 2001-Peter Adorno, 66, of Linwood Avenue. Found dead in his apartment after he was stabbed several times. Stabbing

July 28, 2001-Donald Couitt, 30, of Bucklin Street. Witnesses said he was shot after he exchanged words with men in an SUV. Shooting

Sept 23, 2001-Joseph Hector, 17, of Camp Street. Shot and killed in a drive-by shortly before 11 p.m. Shooting.

Oct 11, 2001-Louis Bruno, 24, of Warrington Street. Was shot in the street and pronounced dead at Rhode Island Hospital. Shooting

Nov 5, 2001-Ernest Tucker, 26, of Admiral Street. Found in the driver's seat of a jeep suffering from gunshot wounds. He was pronounced dead at Rhode Island Hospital. Shooting

Nov 30, 2001-Sigifredo Alarcon, 40, of Branch Avenue. Shot and killed in Benny's parking lot. Shooting

Dec 15, 2001-Jacob Delgado, 19, of Broad Street. Was shot and killed. A second person was wounded but survived. Witnesses said suspect was in his early 20s and either Hispanic or Cape Verdean. Shooting

Dec 16, 2001-Manuel Rodriguez, 24, of Manton Avenue. Was found lying in the road after being shot in the head. Shooting

March 28, 2002- Vaughn Thompson, 33, of Public Street. Found in a parking lot after being shot. Was pronounced dead at Rhode Island Hospital. Shooting
July 27, 2002- Jamal Perry, 17, of Potters Avenue Pronounced dead at Rhode

Island Hospital following shooting. Shooting

July 29, 2002- Jamal Bailey, 24, of Prairie Avenue Crashed his car into a pole after being shot in the head. Shooting

Sept 18, 2002- Gabriel Delgado, 23, of Taylor Street Shot at his home and pronounced dead Rhode Island Hospital. Shooting

Sept 20, 2002- Jermaine Ellis, 12, of March Street. Shot and killed near the Chad Brown Housing Project. Another teenager was also shot but survived. Jermaine's brother was killed in a shooting two months later. Shooting

Nov 16, 2002- Dean Smith, 42, of Potters Avenue Found shot to death in a car. A second victim was shot but survived. Shooting

Dec 1, 2002- Chhouy Chhoeun, 18, of Cranston Street Found shot in the chest. Pronounced dead at Rhode Island Hospital. Shooting

Feb 2, 2003- Glen Rivera, 23, of Chalkstone Avenue Friends drove him to hospital after shooting. Was pronounced dead at Rhode Island Hospital. Shooting

May 14, 2003- Anthony Mitchell, 20, of Hillcrest Avenue Found shot to death in a car. A second victim was shot but survived. Shooting

May 29, 2003- Arleides Tangarife, 23, of Suffolk Street Found dead in driver's seat of car after being shot several times. Shooting

May 30, 2003- Francisco Ortega, 19, of Salmon Street Was found shot in parking lot and later pronounced dead at Rhode Island Hospital. Shooting

June 2, 2003- Albert Burney, 23, of Chestnut Street. Shot and found dead at the scene. Shooting

July 22, 2003-Rafael Diaz, 23, of Manton Avenue Shot in front of a gas station. Pronounced dead at Rhode Island Hospital. Shooting

July 25, 2003-Dion Robinson, 18, of Harold Street Shot on the sidewalk and found inside of a Harold Street home. Pronounced dead at Rhode Island Hospital. Shooting

Sept 13, 2003-Carlos Mendoza, 23, of Hartford Avenue Found in the rear seat of a jeep. Pronounced dead at the scene. Shooting

Dec 13, 2003-John Smith, 77, of Dudley Street Elderly man was beaten by three men in a suspected home invasion. Beaten

Dec 25, 2003-Roy Weber, 22, of Shipyard Street Found on side of the road by Johnson & Wales security officer. N/A

Jan 30, 2004-Deborah Tyrell, 46, of Bucklin Street Shot to death in a convenience store. Shooting

July 1, 2004-James Benevides, 20, of Elmwood Avenue Found dead near the boat house in Roger Williams Park. Shooting

July 8, 2004-Nelson Ayala, 38, of Julian Street Stabbed in the chest and pronounced dead at Rhode Island Hospital. Stabbing

Sept 6, 2004-Bradley Flynn, 21, of Broad Street Shot during fight in front of South Side nightclub. Shooting

Sept 26, 2004-Helene Kramer, 35, of Kinsley Avenue Found dead in apartment. N/A

Oct 22, 2004-Nancy Sousa, 50, of Calder Street Found in apartment in apparent double homicide. N/A

Oct 22, 2004-Michael Sansouci, 40, of Calder Street Found in apartment in apparent double homicide. Shooting

Nov 14, 2004-Jonathan Hernandez, 20, of Hawkins Street Found shot to death. Shooting

Jan 9, 2005- Emanuel Fermin, 27, of June and Berkshire Streets. Found dead in street. Shooting

June 19, 2005- Dwayne Sampson, 26, of Northup Street. Found dead on arrival of apparent gunshot wound. Shooting
June 18, 2005- Shawn Isom, 30, of Grosvenor Street. Found on ground in

parking lot shot at least once. Shooting

August 7, 2005- Fernando Ventura, 23, of Perkin St. and Chalkstone Ave. Found shot in street. Shooting

Dec 23, 2005- Dennis Hayes, 16, of Salina Street Shot. Witnesses brought to station for statements. Shooting

Dec 29, 2005- Tonea Sims, 34, of Cahill Street. Found on floor of her home kitchen with gunshot wounds. Shooting

Dec 30, 2005- Johnny Jimenez, 32, of Cornwall Street. Pronounced dead at the scene. N/A

Feb 21, 2006- Arthur Olink, 23, of Magnolia and Agnes Streets. Found dead after a call for a check of well-being. N/A

Feb 21, 2006- Matthew Cyr, 21, of Magnolia and Agnes Streets. Found dead after a call for check of well-being. N/A

March 5, 2006- Gladys DeVillar, 53, of Hartford Avenue. Found stabbed in chest at Hartford Avenue Laundromat. Stabbing

April 9, 2006- James McLaughlin, 56, of Bailey Court. Stabbed in chest. Died at RI Hospital. Stabbing

August 25, 2006- William Garcia, 42, of Salmon Street. Found dead on scene from several gunshot wounds. Shooting

Dec 25, 2006- Kendall Marshall, 29, of Crary Street. Shot inside Club Pulse. Pronounced dead at RI Hospital. Shooting

Feb 9, 2007- Manuel Lugo, 41, of Petteys Avenue. Suffered an apparent gunshot wound. Shooting

August 25, 2007-Vidal Rodriguez, 33, of Valley Street. Shot outside El Tiburon Club. Pronounced dead on scene. Shooting

October 1, 2007- Luis Abreu, 21, of Ohio Avenue. Found in driver's seat of BMW with apparent gunshot wounds. Shooting

October 5, 2007- Junie Johnson, 21, of Wisdom Avenue. Pronounced dead at RI Hospital. N/A

Dec 21, 2007- Nathan Davis, 25, of Knowles Street. Shot. Pronounced dead at RI Hospital. Shooting

Jan 20, 2008- Michael Holston, 32, of Franklin Square. Found shot inside Jeep in parking lot of Desires. Shooting

March 31, 2008- Angel Vargas, 21, of Allen's Avenue. Shot. Police say black SUV fled incident. Pronounced dead at RI Hospital. Shooting

June 5, 2008- Michael Fortes, 19, of Warrington Street. Suffered single gunshot wound in the back. Victim's mother says she saw a dark-colored vehicle parked outside the house. Shooting

March 3, 2009- Milo Martinez, 20, of Chalkstone Avenue. Shot in head. Victim's girlfriend's vehicle stolen in incident. Shooting

June 12, 2009- Charles Joiner, 27, of Vinton Street. Shot in torso. Pronounced dead at RI Hospital. Shooting

July 6, 2009- Randy German, 20, of Cranston Street. Nearby witnesses say German was shot in torso inside 527 Cranston Street. Shooting

July 11, 2009- Rafael Hernandez, 56, of Broad Street. Found dead during fire suppression. N/A

Dec 6, 2009- David Thomas, 22, of Dorrance Plaza Found shot in vehicle in front of courthouse. Shooting

Dec 6, 2009- Domingo Ortiz, 21, of Dorrance Plaza Found shot in vehicle in front of courthouse. Shooting

Dec 16, 2009- Eugene Briggs, 28, of Thackery Street Suffered two apparent gunshot wounds. Pronounced dead at RI Hospital. Shooting

Dec 24, 2009- David Delacruz, 18, of Congress Avenue Transported to RI Hospital with gunshot wound. Pronounced dead at hospital. Shooting

Dec 31, 2009- Francisco Mendez, 31, of Elmwood Avenue Found lying in street with gunshot wounds. Pronounced dead on scene. Shooting

Jan 15, 2010- Kevron Poston, 20, of Smith Street Shot inside barber shop, Inner-City Hair Salon. Shooting

April 1, 2010- Timothy Kilgore, 25, of Dexter Street and Bellevue Ave. Found lying on the ground bleeding from gunshot wounds. Died at RI Hospital. Shooting

April 27, 2010- Ruben Lopez, 33, of Delaine Street Suffered multiple gunshot wounds. Pronounced dead at hospital. Shooting

May 30, 2010-Lamarr Trisvane, 26, of Donelson Street Suffered a gunshot wound. Pronounced dead at RI Hospital. Shooting

June 16, 2010-Andy Luna, 19, of Elmwood Avenue Shot in torso at Blanco Hair Salon. Shooting

Dec 17, 2010-Ernesto Juarez, 55, of Sorrento Street Wife found Juarez unresponsive on floor. Juarez sustained various injuries including a gunshot wound. Shooting

Dec 18, 2010-Zackary Marshall, 22, of Friendship and Peck
Streets Found unresponsive on sidewalk. Died later at RI Hospital. N/A

June 18, 2011-Jason Rolon Ortiz, 22, of Summer and Haskins Streets Found shot in the parking lot of the Islamic Center. Died on scene. Shooting

Aug 10, 2011-Anthony Stone, 26, of Broadway Street. Found shot in the head. Several witnesses left statements. Shooting

Oct 2, 2011-Steven Latimer, 23, of Dyer Street Suffered several gunshot wounds to torso. Several others shot in the incident. Shooting

Oct 7, 2011-Derek Taylor, 34, of Highland Avenue Found unresponsive in driver's seat of a Chrysler Caravan. N/A

Oct 15, 2011- Pablo Segura, 18, of Hartford Avenue Shot in head. Shooting

Oct 26, 2011- Daniel Thompson, 33, of Broad and Public Streets Found in driver's seat of car, shot in the head. Several witnesses interviewed. Shooting

Nov 26, 2011-Essence Christal, 21, of Broad and Houston Streets Shot in car. Car veered off roadway, hit a tree and rolled onto its roof. Shooting

Nov 28, 2011- Joel Figuereo, 14, of Sumter Street Shot and pronounced dead at scene. Several witnesses interviewed. Shooting

January 3, 2012-Rene Urena, 25, of Lenox Avenue Shot multiple times. Pronounced dead on scene. Shooting

June 5, 2012-Juan Correa Cintron, 38, of Massachusetts Avenue Shot in torso. Others shot in incident. Shooting

June 12, 2012-Devon Young, 21, of Baker Street Shot in head. Several people interviewed. Shooting

June 21, 2012- David Hollis, 38, of Veazie Street and Douglas Avenue Shot. Multiple subjects gave statements. Shooting

August 11, 2012-Robert Ballew, 27, of Palm Court Found dead in driver's seat of Dodge pickup truck. N/A

Sept 8, 2012- Omar Polanco, 19, of Sayles Street Found dead on scene with gunshot wound to head. Police canvassed crowd for potential witnesses. Shooting

Oct 22, 2012- Joel Wills, 40, of Beaufort Street. Found unresponsive with apparent trauma. N/A

Oct 25, 2012 Sandi Fahnbulleh, 36, of Academy Avenue Suffered gunshot wound to upper torso. Died at RI Hospital. Shooting

March 27, 2013 Wesley Smith, 20, of Tanner Street Found lying face down on sidewalk suffering shot to head. Died on scene. Shooting
April 23, 2013 Demitri Todd, 19, of Harvard Street Found 30 feet from car crash, suffering gunshot wounds. Shooting

May 20, 2013 Tyler Marchand, 19, of Steere Avenue Found on ground with gunshot wound to back. Shooting

June 22, 2013 Jose Sanchez, 20, of Clym and June Streets Found in street with gunshot wounds. Shooting

July 4, 2013 Josue Harney, 20, of Henry Street Large street party ended in altercation and shots were fired. Pronounced dead at RI Hospital. Shooting

Note: Six unsolved homicide police reports were unavailable.

THE ESSCENCE T. CHRISTAL MEMORIAL FOUNDATION

In continuance of keeping Esscence's Legacy alive, Kobi Dennis began a collaboration of organizations under an umbrella named Unified Solutions with my nonprofit being named The Esscence T. Christal Female Youth Empowerment Program honoring Esscence. The program would consist of free dinner served for every session, birthday celebrations, and special Occasion dinners. This would-be set-in position to cater to underprivileged, at risk females in the community. The program offered Domestic Violence Prevention/ Support, Mentorship, and Advocacy. Every Wednesday from 6-8 PM. held in 6 week increments with graduations. Our program would prosper so well that we would later be an accredited program to high school students. The females were led with guided conversations on topics for everyday lifestyles. Lisa Scorpio would be the Youth Program Coordinator who was the key to providing the support to our students. She recruited the guest speakers as well as prepared all activities and events for the females. My daughters Antoinette and Keyonna would be the Engagement leads, while Chavon and I would be the Program Educators. Giovanna Rodriquez and Joyce O'Connor were also great assets to the program filling in as Educators when I was unavailable.

Once a month, we would have guest speakers to join us and speak to the females about the topics we had educated the females on the entire month. We would also have professional development on the third Friday, where we would take our youth females out for manicures, pedicures, and special treats to reward them for the great work they were doing in taking in the information and making change in their behaviors and lifestyle.

Successfully, the program has educated and graduated over 60 youth females.

The program was recently implemented in my place of employment where we service students who struggle with their behaviors in regular school environments. My mission was to educate our youth females so that they understood the importance of becoming involved with the wrong individual could end you up severely hurt, abused, or possibly dead.

We have to learn that once a life is taken, there is no coming back. If we are willing to stay silent and call that snitching, then I send a message. Please be ready to continue burying our babies to senseless acts of violence, living in a society of youth who are living in poverty, single family homes, and improper education with the streets being their friends and parents, guns are and will be their new idols. Since no one wanted to do what was morally right, as her mother and her voice, I did not have a problem with walking this path, I openly, boldly, and responsibly told her story!

Esscence and her son Dwayne

Made in United States
North Haven, CT
17 September 2023

41677411R00075